It was the first time
she had shared a bed

But Mark stayed strictly to his own side.

It was still dark when she awoke, jerked from the depths of slumber by the weight of the arm thrown over her waist. Mark had moved the full width of the bed to lie beside her, body turned on one side, breath warm on her cheek. He was still asleep and unaware of his actions.

The arm about her moved, the hand sliding upward to find her breast. Dana froze to the touch—and then as suddenly thawed, coming alive to other awakening senses in her body. He said something indistinctly and rolled over on top of her as he found her mouth in a kiss. Dana responded, aware of his arousal and needing to know more—yearning to know it all....

KAY THORPE

a man of means

Harlequin **Books**

TORONTO • NEW YORK • LOS ANGELES • LONDON
AMSTERDAM • PARIS • SYDNEY • HAMBURG
STOCKHOLM • ATHENS • TOKYO • MILAN

Harlequin Presents first edition February 1983
ISBN 0-373-10573-8

Original hardcover edition published in 1982
by Mills & Boon Limited

CHAPTER ONE

THERE were nine other people at the long mahogany table gleaming with silver and crystal, but for Dana only one familiar face in that of the man seated at the head of it. Even then, after less than a month of her father's regular company, she could scarcely claim to know him so very well. They had been almost total strangers for too many years for the barriers to drop so easily.

At forty-eight he was still an extremely good-looking man, she acknowledged, watching him with green-eyed concentration as he conversed with his right-hand partner: the kind of well-cut, mature looks many women seemed to find so irresistible. Had he wanted it, he could have married again at any time during the ten years since her mother's death—that was already becoming apparent, yet he remained a widower. A tribute to her mother? Somehow she doubted it. Charles Payne simply had no desire to tie that particular knot again. He preferred his freedom.

It was easier in many ways to think of him as Charles rather than Father. Fathers were caring people. They didn't leave their only child to the guidance of others. Dana could count on one hand the number of times she had seen him since she was seven years old, and at that their brief periods together had not been times to recall now with any great sense of nostalgia.

His offer of a permanent home with him had come at a time when, schooling behind her, she had believed herself committed to a life of worthy if dull endeavour in the service of the aunt with whom she had spent the great majority of her holidays. Eleanor Payne was a spinster, devoted to good works in the finest sense. Dana both loved and respected her, but had found no true fulfilment in becoming her helpmate. Never more than an average student, she had been forced to acknowledge, however, that finding a job suited to her capabilities was not so simple. With her father she had one ready-made—or so he had intimated. She was to keep house for him, to organise the dinner parties at which he entertained his business contacts and associates, and act the hostess when necessary. If it occurred to her that her qualifications for such a role were little more than barely adequate, she kept the notion strictly to the back of her mind. What mattered was that her father wanted her with him. If he needed to manufacture a reason then she was more than ready to go along with it, and do her best to live up to his expectations.

Only that wasn't proving so easy either, she admitted to herself now with a small, inward sigh. Years in the confines of an all-girls' school had provided her with little grounding in the art of small-talk, and that was what she so desperately needed to feel at ease in present company. She had tried hard to retain Mark Senior's attention on the occasions when he turned it in her direction, but the woman seated on his other side was more competition than she could handle. More competition than most could handle, she told herself in some attempt at mitigation. Marion Gissard was not only one of the most attractive women Dana had ever seen, she was also mature enough and intelligent enough to be able to meet her companion on equal terms. Small wonder that he found himself unable to tear his eyes away from that smooth oval face under the sweep of blonde hair for very long.

From where she sat, Dana had a distant view of her own image in the large, ornate mirror behind her father's head. Even from a distance she looked so young and unseasoned, she thought depressedly. Long hair was out—especially nondescript, mid-brown hair like hers.

She should have it cut and styled, maybe even lightened. People had told her she was pretty, and she had to believe them, but it was an unremarkable kind of prettiness such as might be found on a dozen other girls her age and colouring. What she lacked was sparkle, and she wasn't at all sure how to acquire it. A new hairstyle only went part way; any radical change had to come from within.

Her left-hand partner was speaking to her now. She made an effort to concentrate on what he was saying, finding him less intimidating than Mark Senior because he was her father's age and failed to stir the same sensations. At thirty-five, Mark was every inch the male of the species, tall and powerfully built in the stark black and white of his dinner suit, with a litheness of movement which bespoke perfect health and fitness. Strictly speaking, he wasn't the handsomest of men, she supposed. His attraction lay in the angles and planes of the taut-featured face; in the crisp dark brown hair clearing his collar to lie in a thick, disciplined line her fingers had ached to touch for the last hour and a half. Feelings like that one were a new experience for Dana. She wanted to savour it, to examine it, to be alone so that she could relive the very first moment she had set eyes on the man who held her father's immediate future in his hands.

Even now she found it difficult to see him for what he was. Bankers were older; grey-haired and grave-featured. At least, that was what she had always believed. Senior & Simpson was one of the oldest and most respected commercial banks in the City. When Joseph Senior died, her father had said, there was little to stand in the way of Mark's claim to the chair. In his present position he was still well able to sanction the loan extension which would pull Payne Enterprises out of deep water. The question was whether he would see fit to do so. Dana could only hope and trust that he would. Her father had worked too long and too hard on this particular project to see it go under for want of a few months.

Coffee was served in the living room by one of the staff hired for the evening. Accustomed to the somewhat spartan standards of her aunt's way of life, Dana had found it difficult at first to settle into the luxurious apartment her father found so necessary to him. Essential dressing, he called it. A man must not only be successful, he must be *seen* to be successful. The apartment was leased, as was the Rolls in the garage below, but they served their purpose, she supposed. Certainly no one in this room could possibly realise how close to financial ruin Charles Payne actually was.

He had told Dana only that afternoon, face reflecting little inner turbulence as he explained the details of a financial miscalculation she couldn't even begin to appreciate in its entirety. Six months was all he needed, he had concluded, and only Mark Senior could give them to him. This evening, it was to be hoped, would put the latter in the right frame of mind to do just that. In a little while from now he would be invited into private conference on some pretext or other and the question put to him. Dana privately thought her father wrong on that score—that a man like Mark Senior would prefer to keep business and pleasure strictly separate—but she would not have dreamed of saying as much. She could only cross her fingers and mentally wish him every success.

It was around ten-thirty when the two men did disappear, and little more than ten minutes after that when they returned. Neither face gave anything away on the surface, but some sixth sense told Dana all was not well. There was a certain hardness about Mark Senior's jawline which had not been there before, an element of bravado in the way her father launched into immediate laughing conversation with the nearest of his other guests.

Mark and his blonde companion left shortly afterwards, his farewells pleasant but distant. It was the signal for a general break-up of the evening, although the leavetaking in most other cases was rather more prolonged and friendly.

At twenty past eleven, with the last guest departed and the temporary staff reimbursed for their services and despatched on their way, Dana poured a stiff whisky and took it across to where her father stood at the long picture window looking out over the night-lit city scene.

'I think you probably need this,' she said with compassion in her voice. 'He turned you down, didn't he?'

It was a moment before Charles turned to look at her, his expression rueful. 'Did I make it so obvious?'

'Not to anyone else,' she assured him swiftly. 'Not even to me—except that I was looking for all the little signs. Did he give you a reason?'

The smile was faint. 'He doesn't have to give me a reason. The loan is redeemable a month from today or the bank forecloses on me.'

'Can you raise the money any way at all?' she asked, knowing the answer even as she said it.

'Not in a month,' he admitted. 'I put too many eggs in one basket. I can work it out, but I need the time. Six months could have done the trick, a year would have been a certainty.'

'I'm sorry,' she said helplessly. 'I really am sorry. What will you do?'

He studied the glass in his hand with a visible hardening of expression. 'Desperate straits call for desperate measures. I still have a card or two left to play.' He looked at her then, a long calculating look as if weighing something in balance. 'What did you think of Mark

Senior from a personal point of view?' he asked disconcertingly.

Too inexperienced at concealing her reactions when taken by surprise, Dana felt the swift colour mounting under her skin. She made a small disclamatory movement of her shoulders. 'He seemed pleasant enough. Not that I had a great deal of conversation with him.'

'So I noticed.' The reply held a certain irony. 'A little feminine charm can go a long way.'

Her flush deepened. 'I think it would take more than simple charm to hold Mark Senior's attention for long.'

'Yes, well, perhaps you're right. The Gissard woman uses every trick in the book.' Charles Payne sounded more admiring than critical. 'Maybe you should study her style.'

'We're not the same type,' Dana pointed out, trying not to let the words hurt her. 'And she's older than I am.'

'Quite a bit.' There was an odd glint in his eyes. 'Youth has its own special appeal.'

Not for Mark Senior, she thought, recalling the way his eyes had rested on her: deep, penetrating blue eyes which saw everything and in her had seen nothing of apparent note. His questions had been those of an adult to a schoolgirl—almost avuncular in their indulgence. If he remembered her at all it would be as a child, not a woman.

Later, in bed, she tried to consider the worst that the immediate future could bring. So far as she knew, if a man couldn't pay his debts he had no recourse other than to declare himself a bankrupt. If that happened everything would go, including this apartment. There would be no place for her in his life, no alternative but to return to her aunt's home.

Unless she could find herself a job, of course. But doing what? All worthwhile jobs these days demanded either experience or higher than average educational qualifications, and she possessed neither. A course at a business training college might stand her in good stead, but where was the money to come from?

Still, it might not come to that, she comforted herself. Her father had declared himself not yet beaten, and she believed him. He would find a way.

There were times during the following few days when she longed to ask if that way had been found, but lacked the courage to broach the subject again without some reasonable opening. There was little to be gleaned from her father's attitude, because he was not the kind of man to wear his emotions on his sleeve, and already, she believed, regretted telling her as much as he had. She schooled herself to await the outcome.

When she thought about Mark Senior now it was with mixed feelings, her loyalty to her father not quite strong enough to sway her into total disregard. Hearing his deep-timbred voice on the telephone that Friday morning was a shock in more ways than one.

'I realise it's short notice,' he said, 'but are you by any chance free tonight?'

'Tonight?' Dana repeated stupidly, too dumbfounded to put on any act. 'Well . . . yes.'

'Good.' He sounded clipped, almost abrupt. 'Would you like to come out to dinner with me?'

'With you?' Her own voice was little more than a whisper. 'I . . . I'm not sure I . . .'

'A simple yes is all it takes,' he cut in as she paused uncertainly. 'Of course, if you don't want to come . . .'

'Oh, but I do!' Her tone was eager—too eager; she made an attempt to modify it. 'I mean, it sounds a nice idea, except that I . . . well, it's rather . . .' Once again she broke off, aware of how feeble she must sound yet unable to say the words she knew had to be said.

'If it's your father's reactions you're thinking about, you don't have to worry,' he came back with an odd dryness. 'I already have his approval.'

Dana drew in her breath sharply. 'Does that mean you granted him the extension after all?' she asked before she could stop herself, and could immediately have bitten off her tongue. 'I'm sorry,' she tagged on in haste, 'that really isn't any of my business.'

'No, it isn't,' he agreed without particular inflection, 'but the answer is yes.'

'Oh, I'm so glad!' She let the relief come through without trying to hide it. 'He won't let you down—I *know* he won't!'

'I think I can say that with your father I know exactly where I stand,' came the level reply. 'I'll pick you up at eight.'

The line went dead. Dana replaced the receiver in its rest with a sense of unreality. Mark Senior wanted to take her out to dinner. But why? Because he found her attractive? Because he wanted her companionship? Considering his lack of interest in that direction the other night it hardly seemed likely, yet what other reason could he have? Perhaps, she thought dazedly, she had made a somewhat better impression than she had imagined. Perhaps, after all, youth did have its appeal to a man like Mark. Whatever the reason, he had asked and she had accepted. Did anything else matter?

Everything else mattered, she realised immediately catching sight of herself in the lobby mirror. What was she going to wear? What was she going to talk about? How on earth did one set about entertaining a thirty-five-year-old banker accustomed to women of Marion Gissard's ilk? Panic threatened to overtake her before common sense reasserted itself. All right, so take one thing at a time. First of all she had to decide what she was going to wear. Certainly nothing in her wardrobe sprang to mind as eminently suitable for an occasion of such magnitude.

She looked at her watch, relieved to see the time was only a little after ten. She had several hours in which to change her image, and she was going to use every one of them. Before the dress she had to do something about her hair. A good stylist should be able to suggest an improvement without being too drastic. She could phone now for an appointment before leaving the apartment. Surely someone would be able to fit her in.

She left a message with Mrs Barratt the daily cleaner in case her father rang, and took a taxi across town to keep her hair appointment at twelve. While not in the ranks of the top establishments, Raynors proved to have stylists who not only knew what they were talking about but were shrewd enough to put customer satisfaction before material gain. Inside minutes Dana found herself talked out of the shorter cut she had first contemplated and into a trim and shape which would enable her to ring the changes with a variety of styles suited to what the dresser was pleased to refer as 'hair of such quality and condition'.

For this evening he swept it up into a deceptively loose coil of curls on top of her head, leaving little tendrils to escape as if by accident about her face and neck. For Dana the main satisfaction was in seeing how it added at least a couple of years to her age.

Finding the right kind of dress was not so simple. After trying on and discarding so many she lost count, she finally settled for a beautifully cut plain black jersey which made the most of her slender curves. With her gold necklet and matching bracelet, and her highest pair of heels, she would hold her own, she thought, viewing her reflection in the dressing room mirror with some satisfaction. She looked very different from the girl Mark had met four nights ago. She even felt different. She hoped he would appreciate the transformation.

It was raining when she got outside again—the cold November rain which could so easily turn to snow. Getting a taxi at five o'clock in the evening was little short of miraculous, but she managed it without receiving one drop of water on her precious hair, conscious of the driver's frankly approving glance as she sank into her seat. If she could impress a London cabbie she could surely manage to make some small impact on Mark. His reasons for asking her out at all were still obscure, but at least she could make sure he didn't regret it too much.

Her father was still not home when the doorbell rang promptly at eight. Dana smoothed down the skirt of the black dress with a nervous hand as she went to open it, resisting the impulse to take a final look at herself in the mirror as she passed. If she wasn't ready now she never would be.

Mark had a finger poised to press the button again as she opened the door, his other hand resting in the pocket of his camel overcoat. No, not camel, she thought irrelevantly as she lifted her eyes from the level of his chest to his face, cashmere. The softness and slight sheen of the cloth told its own story.

'Hallo,' she said with surprising steadiness. 'Come on in. I only have to get my coat.'

'There's no rush,' he said. 'The table is reserved for the whole evening.' Blue eyes skimmed over her, lingering a brief moment on the rounded curve of her breasts revealed by the low V of her neckline with no visible reaction. 'You look very . . . eyecatching,' was all the observation he made.

'I thought it was high time I stopped looking like a schoolgirl,' Dana came back lightly. 'After all, I stopped being one several months ago. Do we have time for a drink before we go?'

'Why not?' He sounded easy enough about it. 'I'll have a straight whisky.'

He had taken off the overcoat and was sitting on the long, low chesterfield closest to the door when she turned round with the glasses in her hand. No dinner jacket tonight, she noted, just a plain dark suit which sat on his broad-shouldered frame the way good tailoring should.

'Thanks,' he said, taking the whisky glass from her. The blue eyes were steady, yet with an expression deep down in their depths she found vaguely disturbing. 'How does it feel to be going out with a man old enough to be your father?'

'You're not,' she protested, then paused uncertainly. 'Well, hardly, anyway.'

'It's biologically possible,' he returned, 'but I agree, hardly likely. Still, I'd like to know.'

Her laugh was meant to be light and unaffected; from her side it sounded totally the opposite. 'I prefer older men.'

Dark brows lifted sardonically. 'You've known so many?'

'No.' She floundered a brief moment, then rallied, sensing some hidden motive in the line he was taking. 'It's an instinct, isn't it? Some girls like older men, the way some men like younger women.'

His smile was brief and dry. 'I doubt if it's quite the same kind of instinct, but I'll let that pass. Come and sit down and tell me about yourself. We have a lot of catching up to do.'

Why? she wondered, and felt the first little spear of doubt run through her. At the same time her feet were carrying her forward to take the seat Mark indicated beside him. This close she could catch the faint masculine scent of aftershave, bringing back memories of the other evening when he had sat by her side for two long hours. Only tonight there was no Marion Gissard to capture his attention. Tonight he was all hers—on the surface at least. "Tell me about yourself," she prompted.

'There isn't a great deal to tell,' he said. 'And I'd rather talk about you.'

Dana forced herself to take the bull fairly and squarely by the horns. 'Why did you ask me out?'

If he was taken aback by the directness of the question

he didn't show it. His gaze wandered over her for a moment, assessing the small, regular features, the tilt of her chin, before coming back finally to meet her own with an expression she couldn't fathom. 'Let's just say I found the inducement totally irresistible. You're a very lovely girl, Dana—never doubt that.'

'I'll try not to.' She was dazzled, too far under his spell to conceal her reactions to his nearness. 'I thought you hardly noticed me the other night.'

His shrug was a disclaimer in itself. 'I had an obligation to my guest for the evening.'

'Miss Gissard is very attractive, isn't she?' Dana observed, trying to sound casual about it.

'Yes, she is.' He said it briefly and without emotion. 'She's also an astute business woman.'

So the relationship could very well be more professional than personal, thought Dana in relief. That made things easier. She felt confidence rise in her. Mark was here because he wanted to be. There was no other reason. He found her irresistible, he had said. Well, she found him so too. What did age matter when two people felt the same way?

That was an evening she was long to remember. The restaurant where they ate had a dance floor and an excellent combo. Held against the broad chest, Dana knew she would never experience anything quite like this again. First love was often reputed to be false, she knew, but this was different. Mark was a man not a callow youth, but someone she could look up to; admire and respect. She could scarcely credit that she was here in his arms, the companion he had chosen in preference to any other this evening.

Shorn of her customary reticence, she found herself telling him things she had never told anyone before, admitting to her hatred of boarding school and the communal life which was so much a part of it, to her shame in lacking the sharpness of mind which might have drawn her father closer to her. Mark listened and watched her, the blue eyes giving little away behind the wreath of smoke from his cigar.

'Your father has a lot to answer for,' he remarked at one point. 'A spinster aunt is no substitute for a family life.'

'It wasn't really his fault,' she defended, already regretting any implied disloyalty. 'He didn't want another wife. Anyway, we might not have hit it off even if he had married again.'

'He didn't necessarily have to marry again to provide a home for you,' Mark pointed out. 'Other men have managed to bring up a child on their own.' His lips twisted suddenly. 'On the other hand, perhaps that wouldn't have worked out so well either. You needed stability if you needed anything.'

Dana was quiet for a moment looking at him, searching his features for a sign to confirm sudden suspicion. 'You don't really like my father very much, do you?' she said at length.

He made no attempt to deny it. 'We don't have a lot in common.'

'Yet you were ready to loan him money.'

'The bank loaned him money,' he corrected. 'Personal feelings don't enter into it. Perhaps they should.'

Dana refrained from asking the obvious question, more than a little afraid of the answer. Whatever the source of controversy between Mark Senior and her father, it was obviously one the former felt able to put to one side where she was concerned. Better to leave it that way. What she didn't know she couldn't worry about.

It was after midnight when they finally left the restaurant. Dana was quiet in the taxi heading homewards, wondering whether Mark intended seeing her again or if tonight had simply been a self-indulgence on his part. His attitude towards her was hardly one of a man bowled over by desire, yet what other construction did she place on his words earlier? Why else would he have gone to so much trouble to see her at all?

She stole a glance at him in the dimness of the cab interior, but read nothing from his expression. She doubted if anyone ever could—not unless he wished them to know what he was thinking. A product of his job, perhaps—or was it more intrinsic than that? She wanted desperately to reach within that outer shell.

They were almost back at the apartment before he said the words she was longing to hear.

'There's a Hallé concert at the Festival Hall tomorrow night. Do you like Grieg?'

'Oh yes!' Right then she would have sworn undying devotion to any composer he cared to mention. 'But surely it's going to be late to get tickets now?'

'I already have them,' he said. 'It's a regular booking. When I don't use the seats myself I let someone else have them. It starts at eight. Would you like to eat first or after?'

'Oh after, please.' She was brimming over with sheer relief. Not only was she going to see him again, but so soon. For a moment it occurred to her to wonder who he might have been taking to the concert if not her, then she swiftly dismissed the thought. She was the one he wanted to be with. He was making that obvious. Why not just accept it and let matters take their own course?

He told the cab driver to wait when they reached their destination and walked her in to the lifts. Conscious of the doorman's speculative gaze on them, Dana found it difficult to take her leave with nonchalance.

'It's been lovely,' she said with diffidence, not quite meeting the blue eyes. 'And I'm looking forward to tomorrow. Goodnight, Mark.'

'I'll see you to the door,' he said, and propelled her gently into the lift.

Dana watched the floor numbers all the way up simply for something to do. With the taxi waiting outside, Mark could hardly be intending to come in for a nightcap, therefore she was going to have to say goodnight all over again in the corridor outside her door. Dared she this time be a little more adventurous in her approach? she wondered. Would the world fall in on her if she reached up and kissed his cheek by way of saying farewell for the night? No, not his cheek, came the immediate thought. It was his mouth she wanted to feel against hers. She had imagined it all evening—so strong and firm, yet gentle too. Not like that of her school friend's brother at the pre-Christmas dance, all wet and sloppy. She shuddered a little at the memory. Of course she had had to pretend she liked it, and summon up some kind of response so as not to hurt his feelings too much, but she had never been more relieved in her life than when it was over and she could make some excuse to get away from him. Boys her own age all seemed to have the same approach to kissing—or so she had gathered from the dormitory conversations overheard during the last year or so of her school life. Lack of experience in them too, perhaps.

In the event, Mark took the initiative out of her hands by kissing her first—a light fleeting pressure which left her yearning for more.

'Tomorrow,' he said. 'And don't wear that dress again. It's too old for you.' He was gone before she could answer, leaving her to let herself into the apartment feeling sadly deflated.

Her father was in the study. He came out on hearing her entry, pausing in the doorway to view her face with a strange little smile on his lips.

'Had a good time?' he asked.

'Yes,' she said, 'very.' She looked at him and hesitated, not quite sure what it was she wanted to ask. 'You knew Mark was going to phone me, didn't you?'

'Yes,' he agreed, 'I knew.'

'And you had no objection?'

'Why should I object?' His tone was level. 'His intentions are strictly honourable.'

'Are they?' Dana couldn't hide the eagerness in her voice. 'What makes you so sure?'

'Because he told me so, and a man like that doesn't lie. Apparently you created quite an impression on him the other night.'

'But he hardly noticed me!'

Charles shook his head. 'You underestimate yourself, Dana. He noticed you all right. You know, when a man gets to his age without having married it's usually because he never found anyone who measured up to his requirements in a wife. Maybe what he really needs is someone young enough and malleable enough to grow into his ideal. Has he asked you out again?'

'Tomorrow.' Dana was looking at him with doubt in her eyes. 'Are you trying to say Mark might want to . . . marry me?'

'I'd say there was a very good chance he's thinking along these lines.' He paused, studying her. 'Would you be averse to the idea?'

It was a moment or two before she answered. 'I barely know him,' she got out at last.

'But you like him?'

'Oh yes.' This time there was no hesitation, her voice soft. 'He's so mature, so considerate.'

'A trait you don't often find in younger men,' her father agreed. 'I think he could be what you need too, my dear. Someone who will give you all the things I found so little opportunity to give you these last few years.' He paused again before adding with emphasis, 'Think about it, Dana, and think hard. I don't somehow see Senior as the type to waste a lot of time once his mind is set on a course of action.'

Dana went slowly along to her own room, closing the

door behind her to stand for a moment in the darkness trying to marshall her emotions into some kind of order. She had to believe that her father could be right in his assessment, because it explained so much. How she felt about it was something else again.

Still in the dark, she cast her mind back over the hours she had just spent with the man in question, recalling every detail of the lean features, remembering with a tremor the touch of his hands when they danced. If what her father said was true, she had it in her power to become an essential part of Mark's life: his wife, his companion. All she would have to do was be as he wanted her to be, to become the kind of wife he needed. Never again would the Marion Gissards of the world be able to look down on her as a nonentity. She would be Mark Senior's chosen woman.

CHAPTER TWO

THE concert was excellent, the audience enthusiastic in its appreciation. Applauding along with the rest as the conductor took his bow, Dana wondered if anyone else in the auditorium could possibly be as wound up as she was tonight. These last couple of hours sitting here beside Mark had been some of the most difficult of her life, despite the distraction of the music. If only he would have touched her hand, shown some sign that he knew she was there, it would have been all right. But he hadn't. He had sat through the whole performance like a man immersed in his own thoughts, to the exclusion of everything else about him—including the music.

She turned to him now as they got to their feet along with the rest of the row, determined not to let his mood affect her too much. 'That was wonderful, wasn't it?' she said. 'Especially the Tchaikovsky. I know one's supposed to outgrow him, but I don't think I ever will!'

The smile he turned on her was ironical in its slant. 'You've hardly had time to outgrow anything yet. Or to experience much either, if it comes to that.'

'But I'm learning.' The words came of their own volition. 'And I'm malleable. That has to make up for a lot.'

'It makes you vulnerable,' he said, 'and that's never good. I gather your father did some talking last night,' he added.

Dana's heart thudded in sudden sickening disillusionment. 'What did he tell you?'

'Just what he told you. Not a man to sit back and let

22

matters take their natural course.' His hand came down
on her shoulder as she opened her mouth to speak again,
turning her gently in the direction of the aisle. 'We can't
discuss it here. I'm taking you home with me.'

Home was in Knightsbridge, a suite of rooms taking
up the whole first floor of one of those tall, gracious
houses left over from the Georgian school of architec-
ture. Unlike her father's apartment, there was little that
was modern or functional about it; the furnishings were
chosen for their individuality, for their fine work-
manship and timeless beauty, many of them antiques.
Seated beside the Adam fireplace eating the supper left
for them by Mark's daily housekeeper, Dana felt more
at ease than ever she had in the past weeks. There was
something comforting in antiquity. It warmed the heart
as well as pleasing the senses.

Mark ate little himself, but insisted she finished before
they talked seriously about anything. Having him there
on the other side of the small, round table gave Dana a
strange sensation. This was what it would be like to be
married; just the two of them together. She could be
happy, she was certain. She could make Mark happy
too. Just let her have the opportunity.

He lit a cigar to go with his brandy once she had
finished eating, drawing on the smoke as if he needed
the calming influence of the tobacco fumes. Lit only by
lamp and firelight, his skin had a bronze sheen, the line
of his mouth a certain sensuality. When he spoke it was
with control.

'Dana, I want the truth. How would you really feel
about marrying a man my age?'

Her reply came without hesitation. 'I'd like it.'

'Why?'

She faltered a little then, unable to maintain complete
composure under the steady gaze. 'I . . . Isn't it obvious?'

His smile was faint. 'There's only one thing obvious,

and that's the eighteen years between us. Wouldn't you prefer a younger husband—if you marry at all?'

She shook her head, on firmer ground now. 'I don't like younger men.'

'So you told me before.' Mark paused, eyes veiled. 'We've met just three times. How can you be so sure about what you feel?'

'Because I am.' Her voice was low but unshaken in its resolve. 'I never felt like this about anyone.'

He looked at her for a moment or two in silence, expression undergoing a subtle change. There was deliberation in the way he put down the cigar and held out a hand to her. 'Come over here,' he said.

She went slowly, making no protest when he drew her down on to his knees. His mouth was only inches away from hers, his eyes assessing her reactions with narrowed appraisal. When he kissed her it was not with last night's fleeting pressure. This was meant to last, and to signify. Dana made no attempt to pull away, responding instinctively to the movement of his lips on hers, to the sensations rising inside her. She stiffened momentarily when he put a hand to her breast, but the sensation that touch aroused was far too pleasurable to be denied. This was the way she had imagined lovemaking to be. She wanted to go on, to know more.

Mark was the one to draw back, standing up to deposit her on her feet with an abruptness that jarred her.

'You're a bundle of surprises,' he said on a taut note. 'Where did you learn to kiss like that?'

'From you,' she said. 'Just now.' She was shaken by the desire to be back in his arms again, looking at him with eyes gone luminous. 'I told you I'd never felt like this over anyone before. Kiss me again, Mark—I want you to.'

'No!' His tone had a sharpness to it. 'I think it's high time I took you home. Wait there while I get your things.'

She hadn't moved when he returned. Only when he held out her coat for her to slide her arms into did she say very quietly, 'I do want to marry you, Mark, I really do. I can learn all the things I'll need to learn. I'll be exactly the kind of wife you want me to be. I don't think I could bear it if you changed your mind now.'

'I haven't changed my mind.' His own voice was rough. 'I can't. I only hope you won't come to hate me one day for doing what I'm doing.'

'Never!' She was smiling again, reassured by his assertion. 'Nothing you could do or say would ever turn me against you!'

There was irony in the blue eyes. 'I'll remind you of that sometime. I trust you won't want a very public affair. The Press are going to make enough of it, as it is.'

'I don't care,' Dana assured him. 'I honestly don't care. We can be married in secret, if you like—or at least only tell a few close friends. I only have my father and Aunt Eleanor to think about anyway.' She paused there, her confidence ebbing just a fraction. 'How is *your* father likely to react?'

Broad shoulders lifted. 'Predictably. He'll get over it. Which just leaves the question of—when?' He gave her no time to form a reply. 'You'd better discuss it with your father. I've a feeling he won't see any point in waiting very long under the circumstances.'

He wasn't on his own, Dana thought. For her it couldn't happen soon enough. Once they were married Mark would get over this sensitivity of his regarding the difference in their ages and start treating her as a woman. She wanted that more than anything in the world. For now, the least she could do was accept the attitude he had chosen to strike if it made him feel any better.

Mark was proved correct in his assumption. Charles saw no reason at all to delay the wedding beyond a couple of weeks. With regard to the size of the occasion, however, he proved remarkably adamant. As his only child, he said, Dana was entitled to the best he could provide, and that was what she was going to have. He would speak to Mark himself, he promised, showing little concern for the latter's viewpoint. In the meantime, she had better start thinking about her dress and all the other paraphernalia that went with weddings.

In the end something of a compromise was effected. The wedding would be a church ceremony and Dana would wear white, but she would have only one brides-maid and the guest list would be limited to immediate family with a few very close friends.

Not that that would stop the Press getting hold of it, Dana knew. Mark was far too well known in the City to have any hope of dodging the publicity that was sure to erupt. He seemed to have resigned himself to the in-evitable, and she sometimes found herself wondering why. For a will like his to allow itself to be overruled there had to be an adequate reason, yet none presented itself. She assured him on a couple of occasions that she herself was not concerned about how large or small an affair it was, but she doubted if he really believed her. Eventually she just let matters ride, telling herself it was only going to be a nine-day wonder after all.

Meeting Joseph Senior for the first time was an ordeal in itself. Mark had warned her that his father's attitude towards the marriage was not one of wholehearted ap-proval, but she was unprepared for the severity of his displeasure when he laid eyes on her in the drawing room of his London house.

'She's little more than a child!' he stormed at his son. 'You should be ashamed of yourself!'

'I am,' Mark assured him dryly. 'Let's just say I can't help myself.'

'Nor I,' put in Dana, with what firmness she could muster. 'And I'm very far from being a child, Mr

Senior.' She kept her gaze level as the banker turned his eyes back to her, refusing to allow him to intimidate her. 'I love Mark, and that's all I care about,' she added defiantly.

'You don't know what love is about,' he came back, but his tone was moderate. 'My son is doing what I'd condemn any man for doing and allowing his judgment to be impaired by a pretty face and a lovely young body. To be frank, my dear, if he takes a wife at all it needs to be one who already knows all the things you're going to have to learn.'

'I believe that's what they call being cruel to be kind,' Dana retorted. 'But it won't work, Mr Senior. Whatever skills I need to acquire I'll do it.'

An unwilling smile briefly crossed the thin, lined face. 'I'll say one thing for you,' he growled, 'you've got spirit. And you're going to need it. I give the two of you a year at the most.'

Dana shook her head, seeking Mark's eyes. 'We'll prove you wrong, won't we, Mark?'

'We'll certainly try,' he said.

Later, over dinner, Dana said tentatively, 'Your father looks older than fifty-seven. Has he been ill?'

He didn't answer right away, fingers twisting the stem of his wine glass. 'He has cancer,' he said at last, matter-of-factly, still not looking at her. 'They give him six months—maybe even less.'

'Oh!' She drew in a distressed breath. 'I'm sorry. Does he know?'

'Yes, he knows.' The blue eyes lifted, the pain in them unconcealed. 'So you see, he isn't going to be around to know whether we make it or not.'

'But we will,' she responded swiftly. 'I know we will!' She reached out and put a hand on his in an effort to communicate her degree of certainty. 'It's going to work out fine!'

'Well, look who's here,' drawled a voice as someone

came to a stop at their table. 'The happy couple themselves!'

Mark had risen to his feet, as fully in command of himself as ever. There wasn't even a flicker in his eyes as he looked down at the blonde-haired woman in the dark green dress. 'Nice to see you, Marion.' He nodded pleasantly to the man hovering at her rear. 'Neville.'

Marion had turned her gaze only briefly in Dana's direction. Now she said pointedly. 'I suppose it *is* true what they're saying?'

'That depends,' Mark came back smoothly, 'on what it is they're saying.'

'That you're getting married.'

'Ah.' He inclined his head. 'Yes, that's true.'

'Congratulations,' put in the other man. There was speculation in the glance he rested on Dana's face. 'You're a lucky man.'

'I think so.' Mark made no attempt to introduce the two of them.

Marion looked at Dana again, a longer look this time and not exactly a friendly one. 'I hope you'll be very happy.'

Dana forced a smile. 'Thank you.'

There was silence for a moment or two after the other couple had passed on. Dana watched Mark from under her lashes, trying to assess his emotions from his expression and failing dismally as usual.

'Marion looked wonderful tonight, didn't she?' she said at last, unable to bear the uncertainty any longer. 'She would have made you the kind of wife your father thinks you need.'

'True,' he agreed without turning a hair. 'But then he isn't the one doing the choosing.' His smile held understanding. 'Don't ever feel envious of older women, Dana. You have time on your side. Did you want dessert, or shall we go straight on to coffee? I have an early appointment in the morning.'

It had snowed in the night when Dana awoke on her wedding day, just a thin sprinkling which lingered on the rooftops only a short time longer than it did underfoot. By ten o'clock the sun was shining and the temperature rising to a slightly more comfortable level, although more snow was expected that night. By all accounts it was going to be a cold, hard winter.

Dressed in the long white velvet gown with its matching pillbox hat and tiny veil, she thought she had never been happier. In less than an hour she was to marry the man she had come to love with all her heart and soul; tonight they would lie together in one bed and shed the restraint of the past two weeks. She longed for Mark's lovemaking, yet felt a little afraid of it too. He was a mature and experienced man. Supposing he found her lack of that quality boring?

Common sense came to her comfort there. If he had wanted a woman of experience he would be marrying one, wouldn't he? Like Marion Gissard, for instance. Certainly the latter would never forgive her for stealing her man right out from under her nose. Dana would not have been human had she not felt a small glow of satisfaction at the thought.

To serve as her only bridesmaid, she had chosen the one schoolfriend with whom she had ever had what might be called a close relationship. Beverley Sanderson was a month or two older, and possessed of the kind of outgoing personality Dana would have liked for herself had she been given any choice in the matter.

'You look lovely,' the other girl said now, straightening the fall of the veil. 'Pity the snow didn't come a bit heavier and stay a bit longer. That really would have completed the picture!'

'It hardly ever does in town,' Dana replied practically. 'Anyway, we're stopping off at the studio for photographs before coming back here for the reception. Daddy wasn't taking any risks.'

'You know,' Beverley remarked, 'that's the first time I ever heard you call your father Daddy. Can it be you finally decided he was deserving of the title?'

Dana laughed. 'Actually, I didn't even realise I'd said it, but I suppose we had to get a little bit closer in six weeks of living in the same apartment. He's been so generous. I have a whole new wardrobe of clothes!'

'Perhaps it's just sheer relief that someone else is taking over the responsibility,' Beverley suggested, tongue in cheek. She waited a moment before adding on a different note. 'Two weeks isn't very long, you know, Dana. You are quite sure about Mark, aren't you? I mean, the way you feel.'

'Totally.' There was a quiet certainty in Dana's voice, a smile in her eyes. 'Stop worrying, Bev. I know what I'm doing.'

'Well, I have to admit he's very macho,' the other girl retorted, reverting to normal. 'Men in their thirties have something seventeen-year-olds don't.'

'Like money and position,' Dana put in, forestalling her. 'It's a lot more than that. He . . .' She stopped and laughed, shaking her head. 'He just makes me feel good, that's all.'

'Not too good, I hope, or tonight isn't going to be much fun for him.' Grinning, Beverley ducked the mock fist Dana aimed at her. 'Seriously, though, you really should be taking longer than a few days for your honeymoon.'

'Mark can't get away right now,' Dana explained patiently. 'I've already told you that. We'll be taking a longer break after Christmas—all being well.' She was thinking of his father as she said it, wondering if he would last out the full six months. Certainly Mark would want to be available should anything happen. 'The family own a plantation on one of the Hawaiian islands,' she added. 'That's where we'll be going. It's run by Mark's brother. Apparently he never had any interest in banking.'

Beverley was busy titivating her long fair hair before the mirror, cheerfully tiptilted nose wrinkled in concentration. 'But he's not the best man, is he?'

'No,' Dana admitted. 'I rather gathered they don't get along all that well. You'll like Leo, though. He and Mark were at school together. He's on the Stock Exchange.'

'Sounds just my type. Chief Bridesmaid's prerogative, and all that!'

This time it was Dana's turn to have her tongue in her cheek. 'I doubt if his wife would see it that way. Anyway, he isn't your type. He's a nice, all-round family man.'

The knock on the door drowned Beverley's reply to that. 'The cars are here, girls,' called Charles Payne from the corridor. 'Is Beverley ready? She'll have to go first.'

'Coming!' Dana sang out for them both. She took up the hand-spray of dark red rosebuds, which picked up the colour of Beverley's own dress. 'I still think it's a bit ridiculous having you travel to the church in a car by yourself. You could have come with us.'

'Intrude on the last moments of father and daughter?' Beverley shook her head. 'Simply can't be done.' She was at the door first, opening it to smile brightly on the man standing waiting. 'Goodness, you do look distinguished, Mr Payne! Men should wear morning suits all the time!'

'You're a born flatterer, young woman.' He was smiling too. His glance went beyond her to the slender figure of his daughter and subtly altered its expression. 'You look very much like your mother today,' he said. 'She wore velvet on our wedding day.' There was a pause, then he briskened again. 'Right, Beverley. I'll see you down to the car, and then come back for Dana. We're in good time, so there's no rush.'

Left alone, Dana took a last lingering glance in the mirror, trying to see herself as Mark would see her in half an hour's time. Mrs Mark Senior. It sounded unbelievably wonderful. She was going to make him proud of her, she vowed. She was going to become the most accomplished hostess in town. People would fight for invitations to their dinner parties. She had to laugh at her own flights of fancy. It wasn't going to be quite that easy. As Mark's father had said, she had an awful lot to learn. But the day would come sooner or later when she could look back on this period of her life and know she had made the transition. It was going to be worth working for.

Her father was very quiet in the car, as if his mind was elsewhere. Dana wondered if he was reliving the day of his own marriage, seeing his bride the way she had looked on that occasion. Dana had loved her mother very deeply. She had been such a gentle person, yet bubbling over with gaiety. Losing her had been a devastating blow, made even worse by her father's decision to send her away to school. Still, that was all in the past now. Today she was to enter a whole new world. Nothing could touch her now she had Mark to look after her.

There were Press photographers waiting outside the church, along with a sizeable crowd of onlookers. Facing the battery of flashbulbs, Dana tried to look confident and unconcerned, as if getting married were an everyday occurrence. Then they were in the church entrance and the organ was switching to the familiar, heart-lifting wedding march, the congregation rising to its feet as she moved at her father's side down the long aisle towards the tall figure of her husband-to-be.

Only when he turned to look down at her did she feel the tension begin to relax. He was as nervous as she was, jaw rigidly set. She smiled at him mistily, relieved to see the taut line soften a little. When he took her hand it was as if all her life she had been waiting for this one single moment.

The ceremony itself went by in a dream. Afterwards, facing the flashing bulbs again, Dana no longer had to put on any conscious act. She was a married woman now, able to face the world on any level. It felt good.

She had thought Mark might kiss her when they were in the car, but he made no attempt. He looked superb in the pale grey morning suit. She could still scarcely credit that he was her husband.

'Happy?' she asked softly, sliding a hand under his.

'Relieved it's over,' he admitted. The blue eyes moved over her face, then down the long, smooth line of her neck to the point of her stand-away collar, expression veiled. 'I'm glad you wore your hair up. You look very lovely.'

And less like a juvenile; he didn't have to say it, she knew what he meant. It was the main reason she had chosen the style.

'I'm getting older by the minute,' she laughed. 'By the time we reach Bembridge I'll be almost middle-aged!'

'On that reckoning, I'll be approaching senility,' he commented dryly. 'There's no magic wand that can age you overnight while leaving the rest of us untouched.'

'In which case, you'll just have to settle for what you've got,' she responded blithely.

'Yes.' There was resolve in his eyes. 'That's what I intend to do.'

CHAPTER THREE

THE photographs took little more than half an hour, after which the bridal party was free to carry on to the reception. Standing in line by Mark's side to greet their guests, Dana thought she had never felt more self-assured than she did at this moment. Even the sight of Mark's double appearing in front of her failed to disturb her equanimity for more than a second or two. No, not quite his double, she realised. This man was eight or nine years younger, his dark hair cut to a more casual style. Apart from that, though, the resemblance was uncanny.

'You have to be Brendon,' she said. 'I'm so glad you could be here!'

'Couldn't miss big brother's wedding day,' he returned easily. 'Anyway, I was due for a break. Must be three years since I took a decent holiday.' His glance moved to his brother's face, the paler blue eyes taking on irony in the process. 'Congratulations. Your taste does the family credit.'

'You might have let me know you were coming,' responded his brother without particular inflection. 'Where are you staying?'

'At the house. Where else?' The tone was casual, the glint was not. 'I'd better move on. I'm holding up the line.' To Dana he added, 'See you later, little sister.'

Dana stole a swift sideways glance at her husband as the younger man passed on, seeing the compression about his mouth without surprise. That there was little love lost between the brothers was fairly apparent. The question was—why? It wasn't even as if they were rivals in business.

It was an hour or more before she got to speak with Brendon again, and only because he made a point of cornering her as she moved between groups of guests.

'Spare me a few minutes to get acquainted,' he said. 'I've a feeling that's all we're going to have.'

Dana looked at him for a long, reflective moment before saying candidly, 'What is it between you and Mark? You act more like sparring partners than brothers.'

'Clashing of personalities,' he admitted. 'We may look alike, but there the resemblance ends.'

'There has to be more to it than that,' she protested.

'All right, so there's more to it than that.' His shrug made light of the subject. 'Get Mark to tell you about it some time.' He paused, studying her, a curious expression in his eyes. 'You know, you're not at all what I anticipated. You can't be more than twenty.'

'I'm not,' she said, seeing no reason to lose three hard-gained years. 'Why should that surprise you?'

'Because Mark's taste in women usually runs to something older.'

'On a casual basis perhaps. Marriage is different.'

'Very. It's harder to get out of, for one thing.'

'Are you married?' Dana asked, struck by something in his voice, and saw the blue eyes flicker.

'I almost was once until she met someone else.' The pause was fleeting but marked. 'Not that she didn't lose out in the end, because he didn't marry her either.'

He was talking about Mark, she was certain. It explained everything. She wanted to ask how long ago it had all happened, but couldn't bring herself to reveal any personal concern. What was in the past was strictly Mark's own business. In no way could it affect them now.

'How long are you staying in England?' she queried instead. 'That's assuming you'll be going back to Hawaii eventually.'

He shook his head. 'I've had enough. I installed a temporary manager before I left. The rest is up to Mark.'

'Don't you mean your father?'

'Not any more. He's handed over control of family finances. In six months Mark will have it all. There's only one other serious contender for the chairmanship, and he's going to be a couple of votes short when the time comes.'

'You can't predict that,' Dana protested. 'No one can.'

'You can when you know the people involved. Not that he'll be a bad choice for the bank. Credit where credit's due.' His sudden grin was infectious. 'No pun intended.'

'None taken,' she quipped back, laughing with him. 'So where do you go from here?'

'I haven't decided yet. I might stay around town for a while.' He hesitated before adding, 'You do know about Father, I suppose?'

'Yes.' Dana sighed as her eyes automatically sought the gaunt figure seated by one of the windows. 'Mark says there's no possible chance of recovery.'

'No, it's gone beyond that. One reason why I'd like to stay around for a time. I've hardly seen anything of him this last three years. One thing is certain, he won't be making any more trips out to Maui.' His glance went beyond her shoulder, his mouth taking on a slant. 'Come to claim your bride?'

'There are others who'd like to speak with her.' Mark sounded curt. 'Why don't you go and do some circulating yourself?'

The shrug was light. 'There's nobody else I find interesting. What happened to Gary, by the way?'

'He couldn't make i ' The curtness was even more pronounced. 'Dana?'

She gave the younger man a small, semi-apologetic

smile before moving away at Mark's side. 'Who is Gary?' she asked, to forestall any other comment he might have to make.

'My youngest brother,' came the unexpected reply. 'He's out of the country.'

Three of them, not two. Dana wondered why that fact hadn't been mentioned before this. Not that it really mattered so much. She had all the time in the world to get to know Mark's family.

Mark's best man had given them the use of his week-end cottage at Bembridge on the Isle of Wight for the duration of their brief honeymoon. Changing her clothing for the journey in the privacy of her former bedroom, Dana mentally blessed the thoughtfulness which had led Mark to use her father's room for the same purpose. Tonight when they were alone together she would conquer her shyness, but for the moment it was undeniably present, and he had recognised the fact. Clad in the jade green jersey dress in which she had elected to travel, she pulled on the full-length blonde mink coat and matching cossack hat which had been Mark's wedding present to her, and saw a stranger in the mirror. Gone the young and ingenuous girl; in her place stood someone taller, sophisticated, even glamorous. The sight gave her confidence in the way no words could have done. If she could look the part she could act the part. Mark's wife. The one he had chosen. She was going to make sure he never regretted that choice.

She was thankful when the leavetakings were over and they were alone in the car heading for the Southampton docks. Dana Payne was dead. She was Dana Senior now, capable of anything and everything.

'What time shall we be there?' she asked as they left the suburbs behind them and took to the motorway.

'Around eight, all being well,' Mark answered without taking his eyes from the road ahead. 'The woman who keeps an eye on the cottage when Leo and Jean aren't

there is going to have a meal ready for us, so we shan't
need to stop on the way. Are you warm enough, or
would you like the heater turned up a little?'

'Oh no, I'm fine!' She snuggled her face into the softness of the fur collar as she said it, loving the feel. 'This
is such a beautiful coat, Mark. It must have cost you
the earth!'

His smile was fleeting. 'No more than it was worth.
Why don't you snatch some sleep? It's been a long day.'

And it wasn't over yet, Dana thought, looking ahead
to the time when they reached the cottage and closed
the door between themselves and the rest of the world.
She wanted that moment very badly because it was only
then that she was going to feel herself really and truly
married to this man at her side. By this time tomorrow
she would know it all: not just the theory but the practice too. Would it change her? she wondered. Would
she feel any different? Time alone would tell.

It was pitch dark when they finally found the cottage
at the end of its own narrow little lane. The caretaker
had left a lamp lit in the deep embrasured window overlooking the front gate, enabling Mark to find the key-
hole with relative ease when they reached the solid oak
door.

Warmth met them as they stepped inside the tiny
lobby from which a flight of stairs curved out of sight
into the upper regions. To the left was a roomy, oak-
beamed sitting room with a well-guarded fire burning
brightly in the natural stone hearth and an inviting
depth to its chintzy sofa and chairs, while to the right
lay the small but adequate dining room with a table
already laid for a meal for two. The kitchen was to the
rear, the heat turned down low on the simmering casserole in its modern oven.

'That smells very good,' Mark commented without
coming further into the room than the doorway. 'I'll

take the cases upstairs while you serve it out—unless you want to wash and change first?'

Dana shook her head. 'It will overcook if we leave it too long. Anyway, I'm terribly hungry. Aren't you?'

'Terribly,' he agreed. 'Five minutes, then.'

Dana left her hat and coat in the sitting room, and went back to the kitchen to wash her hands at the sink before finding an oven cloth and taking the casserole dish from the oven. Two plates already stood in the warming rack above the cooker. She put everything on to a tray and took it through to the dining room, standing the hot casserole dish on a thick mat, then lifting the lid for a quick look. A complete meal in one dish, she realised, seeing potatoes and carrots floating amidst the chunks of brown meat. The aroma was mouthwatering.

Mark came through from the kitchen carrying a champagne bottle. 'I found this chilling in the fridge,' he said. 'Must have been Leo's idea.' He took off the wire and applied pressure to the cork without looking at her. 'I hope you like champagne.'

'On occasion,' she said, and thought how breathless she suddenly sounded. The shyness had returned fullfold. She hardly knew what to say to him. 'How thoughtful of Leo.'

'Yes.' His tone was oddly edged. 'Very thoughtful.'

He was kicking himself for not having thought of it first, Dana realised in quick enlightenment. As if it mattered either way! They were here, they were together, and that was all that mattered. They didn't need champagne to celebrate that fact.

But it helped, she was bound to admit before she was halfway down her first glass. It relaxed her nerves, gave her back her confidence. She looked across the table at the man she had married, feeling the curling sensation deep down in her stomach as her eyes followed the lines of the strong, forceful mouth. In a little while from now she would have that mouth on hers, the warmth of his arms about her. Tonight he would make a woman of her. She could hardly wait for that experience.

As if sensing her regard, Mark lifted his eyes, and for a moment their glances locked and held. There was none of the tenderness she had hoped to see in that gaze, just a hard determination.

'Dana, there's something we have to get straightened out,' he said. 'I know you imagine yourself in love with me, but . . .'

'Imagine?' She was staring at him in astonishment, eyes widened. 'Mark, what are you talking about? I *am* in love with you!'

He shook his head, expression unrelenting. 'Infatuation would be nearer the mark. If often happens with girls your age—particularly where circumstances control a situation. You're a very lovely girl, but there's no way I'm going to take advantage of the way things are.'

'I don't think I understand,' she got out after a moment.

'It's quite simple.' His tone was just as level. 'There are two bedrooms upstairs. We'll each take one.'

Realisation came to her suddenly, bringing a surge of relief because this was something she could handle. 'It's the age thing again, isn't it?' she said. 'You really believe I'm not ready to be a proper wife to you yet. Oh, Mark, that's so silly!' She was smiling, eager to convince him. 'I'm not afraid of the physical side of marriage. I know what it's about.'

'Do you?' There was a tilt to his mouth. 'And where did you get this knowledge from? Books?'

'Partly. We had some sex education at school. There was even a film of . . .' Her voice trailed away before the expression in his eyes.

'So life holds no surprises. That's good. Unfortunately it doesn't have any bearing on the present situation.'

'What situation?' She was sitting on the extreme edge of her seat now, fingers curled tightly about the stem of her glass. 'You wanted to marry me. Why . . .' She broke off again, the colour leaving her face as her mind bridged the gap back to the evening of his proposal—the exact words he had used. When she spoke again it was on a low, uncertain note. 'Why *did* you marry me, Mark?'

'I don't think we need to discuss that,' he said. 'The fact is it's done, and we have to make the best of it.'

'You call this making the best of it?'

'I call it the only possible compromise.' He sighed suddenly, pushing his own glass away from him. 'Dana, you have to accept things the way they are. I can't explain.'

'You *have* to explain!' Her eyes were dark in the pallor of her face. 'You can't just leave it like that.' She hesitated, not wanting to believe the suspicion pressing into her mind yet unable to shut it out. 'It has something to do with my father, doesn't it?'

His regard narrowed faintly, but that was the only reaction he showed. 'What makes you say that?'

'Because he was the one who planted the idea in my mind that you might want to marry me. He was the one who phoned you next day and made sure you put the question to me.' She drew in a shaky breath. 'Why, Mark? Why did he do it? Why did *you* do it?'

He said flatly, 'If you must have it in black and white, it was part of the price I had to pay for his silence. And don't ask me about what, because I'm not prepared to tell you.'

Shock held her rigid for a long moment. When she spoke her voice was a whisper. *'Blackmail?'*

'Of a kind.' His lips widened mirthlessly. 'He needed that loan extension very badly.'

'But you'd already granted that before you rang me that first time.'

'I told you that was part of the price. Our marriage

was his guarantee against anything going wrong. Few men would be willing to bring charges against their wife's father.'

'You could have got out of it,' Dana said, still fighting for control. 'You could have made yourself so unpleasant that I'd have turned against the idea myself. He couldn't have forced me into marrying you.'

Mark smiled dryly. 'I did once start making love to you with the intention of frightening you so thoroughly you'd run like a rabbit, only you refused to be frightened. Anyway, I reasoned that married to me you'd at least be out from under his influence.'

'Such noble concern!' It was her turn to mock, the bitter hurt beginning to seep through every part of her body. 'And what kind of influence am I under now, I wonder? After all, for blackmail to be effective there has to be something the victim can't afford to have known. Is your bank *really* so solid, Mark?'

White skin showed briefly about his mouth as his jaw tensed. 'It has nothing to do with the bank,' he said. 'It's a personal matter.'

'All right,' she challenged, 'tell me about it. I'm as involved as anybody.'

'I said no.' There was no mistaking the note of finality. 'You're just going to have to live with it as it is.'

Dana got to her feet, her limbs shaky. 'I won't do that. Neither will I stay here in this place with you.'

'You don't have anywhere else to go,' he came back. 'Even if you had I wouldn't let you. I realise it's all been a shock for you, and I'm sorry, but it had to be said. You'll soon get over what you fancy you feel for me.'

'I'm over it now,' she retorted with vehemence. 'I hate you, Mark! More than I ever hated anyone in my whole life!'

'You'll get over that too.' He sounded totally unmoved. 'You're my responsibility now, and I intend fulfilling it.'

'I won't let you!'

'You can't stop me. You're still under age. If you try running away I'll have you brought back.' He paused there, face softening just a fraction. 'Dana, I don't want to hurt you any more than you've already been hurt. We can be friends—a brother and sister relationship. Later, when circumstances have changed, we'll see about having the marriage annulled. It shouldn't be too difficult. By then you'll be of an age to manage your own life, and I'll make sure you're well able to do it.'

'With money, you mean?' She shook her head emphatically, hair falling about her face. 'I wouldn't take a penny from you!'

'You'll have time to change your attitude,' he said. 'Why don't you sit down and finish your supper?'

'I'm not hungry.' She moved unsteadily towards the door. 'Right now I'd rather be on my own.'

He made no attempt to stop her. 'Yours is the room on the left.'

Somehow Dana forced her feet to carry her up the narrow stairs and through the door he had indicated. Her suitcase stood ready and waiting on the ottoman at the foot of the double bed with its gay patchwork quilt. She stared at it numbly, thinking of the filmy white garment which lay just under the closed lid. Bought for her wedding night, only there wasn't going to be any wedding night. Mark didn't love her. He didn't even want her. She was on her own, in every last sense of the word.

CHAPTER FOUR

THERE were no tears during the long, lonely hours following, nor even any desire for them. It was as if something in her had died back there in that room when Mark had delivered his coolly prepared little speech, leaving a blank hole where her emotions should be.

She slept eventually, awakening to a crisp clear morning and a resolve which showed no sign of weakening as she showered and dressed in beige cord slacks and sweater. Before anything else was said or done she was going to know just what kind of hold her father had over Mark. He owed her that much honesty at least. If she had to force his hand she would do it without compunction. If one learned from one's parents, then her father had set her an example to follow.

With her face free of make-up and her hair brushed down about her face, she looked too young and too vulnerable. She twisted the latter up into a casual knot and added a dash of bright red lipstick to a mouth already hardened by determination. She wasn't a pawn to be pushed around; that was something both Mark and her father were going to discover.

He was seated at the kitchen table reading the morning newspaper when she went down, a coffee cup at his elbow. Unlike herself he had not yet dressed, his legs pyjama-clad beneath the short silk dressing gown, his feet pushed into leather slippers.

'There's plenty more in the pot,' he said without lifting his eyes from the page. 'Help yourself.'

Dana did so, wondering if coffee was all he had for

breakfast. Even her father had liked to start the day on a well-filled stomach.

'I like to come round slowly when I have the time for it,' he tagged on smoothly, almost as if he had read her thoughts. 'Coffee first, then breakfast proper.'

Dana brought her own cup across to the table and sat down opposite him. She felt nothing because there was nothing to feel. Not any more. All she wanted was the truth, and it was what she was going to have.

'That's good,' she said without particular inflection. 'It gives us time to talk.'

Mark looked at her then, taking in the cool composure of her features with a lift of his brows. 'I was under the impression it had all been said.'

'No, it hasn't.' She paused a moment, choosing her words with care. 'You refused last night to tell me what threat my father was holding over your head.'

'True,' he agreed. 'I still do refuse.'

'Except that this time I'm not asking.'

His stillness was unnerving—or would have been once. Right now Dana found herself able to view him with almost clinical detachment.

'Are you threatening me?' he asked at length.

'If necessary.' Dana held his gaze without flinching. 'Like father, like daughter. If you won't tell me I'll ask him, and if he won't . . .' the pause this time was purely for effect . . . 'I'll go to *your* father and tell him the whole story.'

The strong mouth had tightened into one thin line. When he spoke his tone was low and hard. 'I think you'd better go back to bed and do some reconsidering.'

'I'm your wife,' she pointed out, not moving. 'That, in the eyes of the law, makes me an adult, not a child. You don't send an adult to bed.'

'I wasn't sending you,' he advised in the same deadly tone. 'I was suggesting it might be the best place to be.'

'It should have been,' she rejoined with deliberation. 'Or so I'd been led to understand. Perhaps I've been spared the disappointment of finding it's all overrated anyway.'

The anger went from him suddenly. He ran his fingers wearily through his hair. 'Dana, I know what I did to you was inexcusable, but don't let it sour you for life. You're young, you have it all ahead of you. Once we've got this mess sorted out you'll be free to meet someone else, someone more your own age.'

'I'm sure you're right,' she said. 'Only that's then and this is now.' She kept her voice steady with an effort. 'I meant what I said, Mark. I really will go to your father if I have to.'

The pause seemed to stretch for ever. Dana wondered at her ability to just sit there waiting. There was no telling what Mark was thinking because his face was totally without expression. He just sat looking at her with cold blue eyes.

'I believe you,' he said at length. 'Which doesn't seem to give me much choice. You learn very quickly.'

For a brief, fleeting moment Dana regretted starting this, but only for a moment. Whatever it cost him to admit the truth, it was no more than he deserved.

'I have very good teachers,' she rejoined.

He ignored that, his only sign of tension in the faint contraction of the muscle along the line of his jaw. 'You asked me yesterday about my brother Gary. I told you he couldn't come to the wedding because he was out of the country. That was true, so far as it goes. At present he's being dried out in a Swiss clinic after causing the death of a young girl while driving under the influence of drugs. I'm not sure how your father got hold of the information, because he isn't registered under his own name, but get hold of it he did. He threatened to release it to the Press if I didn't comply with his demands.'

Dana said softly, 'And that wouldn't do the bank's image any good.'

'More to the point, it would kill my father. Gary's twenty-two, the baby of the family—the apple of his eye. My mother died giving him birth, which makes him doubly protective. Gary started kicking over the traces in his teens, but we always managed to keep it from him. I intend to keep right on doing that, as long as he's still with us.'

Dana drew in a long, slow breath. 'And Gary? Will he be facing charges?'

'Not for some time. He was injured himself. When the case does come up . . .' the pause held deliberation . . . 'well, a good lawyer can work miracles.'

'You don't think he deserves to go to jail for what he did?'

'What he deserves and what might do him good are two different things. In jail he'd be confined with just the kind of people he doesn't need. When the time comes he'll go out to the Maui estate and learn about management. That should keep him out of trouble for a year or two.'

'If he stays. At twenty-two he can hardly be forced.'

'He'll stay.' The intonation was flat. 'Anything else you'd like to know?'

Dana shook her head, feeling a little sickened. If both Mark and her father had failed to come up with the truth would she really have gone to Joseph Senior? she wondered. Easy enough now to deny it, but who was to say? At least she would never have that on her conscience.

'I can't condone my father for doing what he did,' she said at length, 'no matter how desperate he was. But I blame you too. He'd have settled for the loan extension if you'd held out.'

'He might,' Mark agreed. 'Although he saw the marriage as a means of safeguarding his interests, as I told you last night.'

'And you believed I'd be safer in your care than in his anyway,' she added, unable to resist the dig. 'The brother of a drug addict!'

She was sorry the moment she had said it, but the apology stuck in her throat before the look in his eyes. When he answered there was no doubting his seriousness.

'Dana, no matter what I've done, if you ever use that term again in reference to Gary you'll regret it more than you ever regretted anything in your life. Is that clear?'

'As crystal,' she retorted. 'Only you're wrong. I'll never regret anything more than ever setting eyes on you in the first place!' She pushed herself to her feet. 'Considering your father's state of health, and *only* because of that, I'll accept things the way they are for now. Just don't expect me to put on any act in public, though. I don't think I could go that far.'

'You won't have to,' he promised tautly. 'I'll see to it that people realise we want to be alone together these first few weeks.'

The irony of it caught her by the throat. Only a few hours ago she had wanted that very thing. Now she only wished she need never see the man she had married again. She left him abruptly.

It was gone lunchtime before he came to see her out, viewing her from the bedroom doorway with hard eyes.

'This has gone on long enough,' he stated. 'You barely ate anything last night, and you only had coffee this morning. I've made you an omelette. Are you coming down to eat it, or do I carry you?'

'I'll come,' she said, knowing he meant it. 'I don't want you touching me!'

'Then don't make me have to. Like it nor not, we're stuck here for another three days, and we're going to spend them like civilised human beings. After you've eaten we're going out for a walk. Tonight we'll find somewhere to have dinner.' He turned to go, adding over his shoulder, 'You've got exactly two minutes.'

She followed him down; there was little point in defiance. The omelette proved to be surprisingly good, her hunger too real to need any pretence. Mark stood at the kitchen window while she ate, hands thrust deep into the pockets of his tweed slacks. In the rough white sweater he looked very different from the well-dressed banker she had hitherto known. Strangely, it was a look that suited him better.

'Do you often cook for yourself?' she asked into the silence which lay between them. 'You make an excellent omelette.'

He turned then, leaning his weight against the unit side as he looked across at her. 'I'm accustomed to making my own breakfast at weekends. Weekdays I prefer to leave early and eat out.'

'There won't be any need for that in future.' Dana was gratified to note the steadiness of her voice. 'I can cook.'

It was a moment before he answered. 'There's no obligation.'

Her shrug was indifferent. 'With Mrs Powell coming in every day I'm going to have little enough to do as it is. At least let me feel I'm giving some small return for my keep.'

The blue eyes glinted suddenly. 'Don't try getting at me that way,' he advised. 'You'll be costing me no more than you would have been under other circumstances.'

'Except that the investment carries a much lower interest rate,' she responded, pleased with her own turn of phrase. 'What's going to happen if you meet someone you really want to marry while you're still tied to me?'

Something flickered across the lean features. 'That would be my concern. Whatever happens, you'll be taken care of.' His tone briskened. 'If you've finished get your coat. I think we could both do with a breath of fresh air.'

The day was fine but cold, the sea grey and unininviting. Shorn of its summer garb, the harbour looked deserted. They met only one other couple on their walk around the perimeter road, exchanging no more than a bare greeting. There was little conversation between them because there was nothing to talk about. As Mark had pointed out earlier, it had all been said.

The warmth of the cottage welcomed them back. Dana made tea and buttered some scones she found in the bread bin, taking the tray through to the sitting room where Mark was listening to the radio.

'We're in for a rough night,' he announced. 'There's a gale warning out. We'll make dinner early so as not to get caught. Leo said the only places left open at this time of year were in Ryde—that's only fifteen minutes away by car.'

'Do we have to stay away the whole four days?' Dana asked tentatively as she poured the tea. 'It all seems rather pointless now.'

'It may do, but we're staying anyway.'

'Why?' she demanded, ignoring the danger signals. 'Because of what people might think?'

'If you like.' He reached out and lifted his cup, mouth unrelenting. 'It doesn't matter why, just settle your mind to the fact that we're staying on. And don't keep challenging me, Dana.'

'Just accept that what you say goes?' She pushed the hair back out of her eyes with a rough little gesture. 'It seems I just exchanged one father for another!'

'With the difference that I mean everything I say exactly the way it sounds,' he came back with purpose. 'Start thinking of me as an older brother, one who cares a great deal about your welfare but isn't prepared to put up with just any attitude on your part. I'll have your respect if I have nothing else.'

Her voice came low. 'How can I respect a man who's done what you've done?'

'By appreciating his dilemma for a start. Would you prefer that I'd gone to the police?'

'No,' she agreed unwillingly.

'That's perhaps as well, considering I didn't have any real charges to bring. What your father was threatening to release to the Press was only the truth. He couldn't have been stopped.'

'You're both of you morally guilty,' she said. 'You extended a loan to him knowing he's far from a good risk.'

'The bank isn't at risk.' He said it quietly but with enough emphasis to lift her head. 'I went guarantor for the whole amount.'

It took her a moment to find the words. 'I didn't realise. I'm sorry.'

'You don't have to be sorry,' he said. 'None of this is your fault. All I'm asking is for a little effort on your part to make the best of what we have.'

'For how long?' she got out. 'I'll be eighteen in February.'

'By which time my father could well be gone.' He said it matter-of-factly. 'Give it till then, at least.'

Afterwards it would no longer really matter all that much to him, she gathered, and felt something harden again inside.

It was an effort to think about getting ready to go out later, but Mark was adamant. Rain was falling when they went outside to the car, the wind already rising. Huddled in her seat as they drove along the dark, wet roads, Dana wished herself anywhere but this place, this time. Yet would have anything changed a month from now? She doubted it. Nothing could change while Mark's father was alive, and one could hardly wish him dead.

They ate an indifferent meal in a sparsely occupied

restaurant served by a solitary waiter who looked as if
he would far rather be hibernating along with the rest
of the island. By nine o'clock they were on their way
back to Bembridge through the driving rain, travelling
slowly of necessity because the windscreen wipers could
scarcely cope with the flow. The wind came in gusts
that rocked the car and tore whole branches from the
trees, growing stronger all the time. Dana hated wind.
It made her edgy and nervous. And it was going to get
worse before it got better, according to the forecast. A
wild night lay ahead.

Just the other side of St Helen's they almost crashed
into an old MG parked at the edge of the narrow roadway just around a bend. The vehicle was in darkness
and looked abandoned; how recently was only appreciated when the headlights picked out the two figures
a few hundred yards farther on. They had stopped on
hearing the car engine and were frantically waving.
Mark pulled to a halt and reached back to unlock a
rear door, letting in a blast of cold wet air along with
the pair of them.

The newcomers were young and looked like students,
their jeans and anoraks already soaked through.

'Thanks a million,' said the girl with real gratitude.
'We didn't think anybody else would be mad enough to
be out in this lot!' She was slicking back long fair hair
as she spoke, dripping water on to the upholstery. 'Sorry
about the mess.'

'Like two drowned rats,' the young man with her
commented cheerfully. 'Trust Myrtle to pick a time like
this to run out of petrol! Do you happen to know where
the nearest garage is?'

'Bembridge,' Mark answered. 'But they won't be open
for service at this time of night.' He put the car into
motion. 'If you'll tell me where you're heading for I'll
take you. You can fetch the car in the morning when
this will, let's hope, have abated a little.'

'That's good of you. As a matter of fact, it shouldn't be too far, from what we were told. Does Rose Cottage mean anything to you?'

'Rose Cottage?' It was Dana who spoke, her voice sharpened.

'That's right. Actually, it belongs to some people called Manston I . . . that is, we got the loan of it for a few days.'

Mark was the first to break the small silence. 'From Leo himself?,

'Well, no.' The younger man sounded faintly perturbed, sensing something not quite right. 'We're both reading Economics with Julian. He said his brother never used the place after October, but wouldn't mind if we did. He even told me where to find the spare key.'

'Generous of him.' There was irony in the comment. 'Obviously it didn't occur to him to check with his brother first.'

'Well, no, as I just told you the family never use the place after——' He broke off, drawing in a slow breath of dawning suspicion, 'I say, *you're* not Leo, are you?'

'That would be a bit too much of a coincidence,' Mark agreed. 'No I'm not Julian's brother, but I do happen to know him pretty well.'

'Oh!' The other sounded nonplussed.

'Look, we're not going to do any damage while we're here,' put in the girl on a slightly belligerent note. 'We just wanted—well, to be on our own for a day or two.'

'In the middle of term?' Mark's tone was deceptively mild.

'Slack period,' Julian's friend had rallied again. 'Like Cathy says, we're not going to do any harm. I'm Ian, by the way—Ian Rodgers.'

'We're already staying at the cottage.' Dana thought it high time someone made that fact clear. 'On Leo's authority, not Julian's.'

'Oh, lord!' There was no doubting the total consternation in Ian's voice. 'That's really torn it! They've stopped the ferries too. We came over on the last one.' He paused, obviously racking his brains for a solution. When he spoke again he sounded more than a little sheepish. 'You wouldn't know somewhere we could put up for the night, would you? It will have to be cheap. We—er—didn't bring very much money with us.'

Dana knew what Mark was going to answer even before he said it. There was very little choice. 'You won't find anywhere at this hour at any price. Most of the hotels and guesthouses are closed for the winter.' The pause was brief. 'You'll have to spend the night at the cottage. There's nothing else for it.'

'Sorry.' Ian sounded subdued. 'I feel an absolute Charley!'

'It isn't our fault.' Cathy was obviously made of sterner stuff. 'I'll half kill that Julian when we get back!'

Dana wished she could have the same opportunity. Leo's younger brother had put them all in a bad spot. The thought of having others know of the situation existing at the cottage made her curl up inside, yet how could they hope to conceal it? Where did Mark think the other two were going to sleep anyway?

She was silent all the way to the cottage, dreading the moment of entry, the necessary prevarications and total lack of understanding. Perhaps they could pretend they really were brother and sister rather than husband and wife, she thought wildly at one point; that would explain the use of both bedrooms. She wondered how Mark himself was feeling about the looming problem. Or did he simply not care? Certainly there was nothing to be gleaned from his expression, or what she could see of it in the darkness. His whole concentration was on the road ahead.

They had left a light in the sitting room. The sight of it beaming thinly through the rain made her want to turn tail and run. Mark parked the car as close to the door as he could get and got out first to unlock it, standing there holding it open against the tearing strength of the wind until Dana and the other two were indoors.

'What a night!' exclaimed the girl called Cathy, sliding out of her sodden anorak. 'Where can I put this thing to drip?'

'Try the kitchen,' Mark advised. 'Show them, Dana, while I get some towels. They're going to need dry clothes too. I can fix Ian up if you'll do the same for Cathy. You look about the same size.'

Dana forced a smile as she met the other girl's eyes. The same size if not the same age. Cathy looked around twenty, with all the confidence acquired from two years of university life. 'The kitchen is back there. I'll find you some jeans and a sweater to put on. Would you like a hot bath before you change?'

'Sounds great. I'll come right up.' Cathy dumped the anorak into Ian's arms. 'Stick that with yours, will you, love.'

'Sure.' He too had recovered his poise, then features cheerful beneath the thatch of light brown hair. His glance lingered a moment on Dana's face, frank appreciation in his smile. 'Nice to be inside out of it, especially with walls as thick as these. At least we'll get a good night's sleep.'

Dana turned away before he could see any change of expression in her eyes. That problem was still to be faced.

Mark came out from the bathroom as they reached the head of the stairs. He was carrying a large thick towel and had a pair of slacks and a shirt over his arm.

'I started the bath running,' he said to Cathy. 'Your friend will have to make do with the fireside.'

'More than he deserves,' she pronounced, 'considering he was the one who let us run out of petrol in the first place. Thanks for taking us in like this—I'd hate to have spent the night in the car.'

Dana waited until the bathroom door was securely closed before saying it. 'Where are they going to sleep?'

'In a bed. Where else?' Mark met her gaze levelly. 'My room will be easiest to clear. Start taking things through while I get these down to Ian.'

She stood without moving, watching him descend out of sight around the bend in the stairs, her mind going around in circles. There was one bed in her room, and only one. Did he really think she was going to share it with him under these circumstances? Why take it for granted that Cathy and Ian had any right to a bed of their own anyhow? The way they lived was their own affair, but that didn't mean one had to condone it.

Mark came back before she could bring herself to start obeying his instruction. He made no comment, simply taking her by the elbow and drawing her into the bedroom he had occupied the previous night. It was the same size as her own, with the double bed covered by a very similar patchwork quilt. Mark opened the wardrobe and took out several garments on hangers, holding them out to her.

'Take these through to the other room,' he said. 'I'll bring the rest.' His mouth firmed when she failed to move. 'Dana!'

'Why should we have to pretend just because those two are here?' she demanded on a tremulous note. 'And how are we supposed to—manage?'

'We'll manage.' There was no softening of resolve in his face. 'Are you going to get hold of these?'

'Frightened they might think you think you're odd or something for not sleeping with your wife?' The taunt came without conscious prompting, born of a need to get through that armour he wore. 'Is it masculine pride at stake?'

'My pride took a beating these last few weeks,' he said without lifting his voice. 'If you want to keep yours intact you'd better start curbing that tongue of yours a little. What those two might think about our relationship from a personal point of view doesn't worry me, what they might tell Julian, and through him, others, does. My father found our marriage alone difficult enough to accept. There's no way I'm going to take even the slightest risk of having him learn that things aren't quite what he took them to be. So, tonight we share a room. A room, I said, not a bed. Now, are you going to take these off me?'

She did so, turning without a word to cross the narrow landing into the other room and lay the garments on the bed. They would have to be hung away later, she thought numbly. Right now it was only necessary that they leave a clear room for their visitors. Where exactly Mark was planning to sleep she wasn't quite clear. The chair perhaps, although it would hardly be comfortable.

He came in behind her, carrying the rest of his things along with the brown leather suitcase.

'That's the lot,' he said. 'Luckily I didn't bring much with me. What about coffee for everybody? And we'd better find out if those two have eaten.'

'They didn't have any luggage,' said Dana without looking at him. 'Do you think they left it in the car?'

'They're probably wearing all they've got with them, but we can always ask. I'll slip back and get it if necessary.'

Cathy was still in the bath when they went downstairs; Dana could hear the slapping sound of water against the tub sides as she moved. She left the clean clothing outside the door. Ian greeted them from the sitting room where he was ensconced on the sofa in front of the roaring fire, long legs stretched before him.

'This is sheer bliss,' he said. 'I hung my jeans over a chair in the kitchen. My shirt was okay.'

Dana left Mark to entertain him and went through to make the coffee, only to return moments later to see if food was also required. They'd had a meal before boarding the ferry, Ian admitted, but a sandwich or two wouldn't go amiss. Dana opened a tin of ham from the cupboard and made a plateful, taking it through along with the coffee to find Cathy already down and drying her hair in front of the fire with a total lack of self-consciousness.

'There's nothing to fetch,' she was saying to Mark as Dana came in with the tray. 'I just stick a toothbrush and comb in my pocket when I'm going anywhere. Saves a lot of hassle. Ian does the same, don't you, love?'

'Slobs,' he agreed, 'the pair of us. Anyway, Myrtle doesn't have much luggage space.' He took a couple of sandwiches from the plate Dana held out. 'Thanks. I'm ravenous! Must be the weather.'

Cathy refused the food but fell on the coffee, draining the cup and looking for more before Dana had time to take more than a couple of token sips at her own.

'Just listen to that wind!' she commented with the refilled cup in her hand. 'Glad I'm not out in it.' She sipped at the liquid this time, eyes roving speculatively from Dana to Mark and back again over the rim. 'Taking a late holiday?'

'Honeymoon.' Dana used the word deliberately. 'We were married yesterday.'

If she had been hoping to disconcert the other girl she was to be disappointed. Cathy simply laughed and shook her head. 'We really did barge in, didn't we!'

Ian was the one who looked discomfited. 'Sorry again,' he said.

'Don't worry about it,' Mark advised without irony. 'Have another sandwich.'

Ian did so, obviously finding some solace in the act of eating. 'We don't even know your name,' he remarked after a moment or two.

'It's Senior.' Cathy's tone was bland. 'Mr and Mrs

Senior. There was a photograph in last night's paper. I wasn't sure until just now.'

'Not like you to read up on weddings,' said Ian, sounding surprised.

'Ah, but this one was rather more prominent than most.' Her eyes met Mark's with an impudent little sparkle. 'You're quite an important man, it seems. "City Banker Weds" was the caption. You've got a brother called Gary, haven't you? I met him a couple of times with Julian Manston. What happened to him, by the way? Julian says he hasn't seen him for months.'

'He's out of the country.' Mark's tone gave nothing away. 'How did you connect the two of us?'

'Julian told me his father and elder brother were in banking—Senior & Simpson. That was what caught my eye last night.' She laughed again. 'Who'd have expected to meet up with you both down here!'

'Who indeed,' Mark said dryly. 'Fate moves in strange ways.' He leaned forward to put his cup on the tray. 'When you're ready, the spare room is on the right at the top of the stairs.'

'Thanks.' Ian sounded diffident. 'You're sure it's okay?'

Dark brows lifted. 'That's your own affair. Leave those, Dana. They can wait till morning.'

'I'll see to them,' Cathy offered as Dana straightened from her attempt to take up the tray. 'The least I can do.'

Mark didn't argue with that. 'Put the guard around the fire before you come up, will you,' he said. 'The last thing we need is a flying spark.'

CHAPTER FIVE

DANA preceded him up the narrow stairway, too well aware that they were going to be the subject of discussion downstairs for some time to come. Cathy was no fool. She recognised all was not quite right with the newly weds if Ian did not. With any luck she would eventually put it down to their own presence and forget about it. Dana only wished she could school herself to do the same.

With Mark in it, the bedroom seemed smaller, more closely confined. Dana gathered up her nightclothes and departed for the bathroom, leaving him to sort out the sleeping arrangements for himself. She could hear the low murmur of voices as she crossed the landing. Without pausing to think about it, and quite without conscience, she crept part way down the stairway to the bend, straining her ears to pick up the words.

'I tell you there's something odd about it,' Cathy was saying. 'Does he look the type to pick up with a kid just out of school?'

'No,' came the rejoinder on a more hesitant note. 'But who's to tell what people are really like underneath? She's certainly got everything in the right places!'

Cathy snorted audibly. 'So have a lot of others, idiot—and better developed too!'

'Okay, so maybe he had to go back that far to find a virgin.' There was just a touch of acidity in Ian's voice. 'Some men are peculiar that way when it comes to settling down.'

Dana stayed to hear no more, noiselessly remounting

the stairs with cheeks burning. A virgin fresh out of school; was it so obvious to everyone? If so, she had to do something about cultivating a different look. To live with the facts of her marriage was one thing, to have others aware of nonconsummation quite another. Yet how did one acquire the look of experience without the practice? What kind of changes did fulfilment bring? Perhaps she should study Cathy's face in the morning and try to analyse what she saw there.

She lingered in the bathroom as long as she reasonably could, returning at last to find Mark already wearing pyjamas and dressing gown.

'I thought you'd decided to sleep in there,' he said mildly enough, getting up from the chair where he had been sitting waiting. 'I'm afraid I've had to take one of the blankets off the bed. I can't find any spares.'

Dana made no answer as he went out of the room. So he really did intend using the chair for the night. It meant he would be getting very little sleep. She looked at the double bed for a long moment, trying to think logically about all this. They were husband and wife, legally if only in name; he had a perfect right to share her bed. They didn't need to touch. It was more than wide enough for two. How could she condemn him to an uncomfortable chair?

She was in bed, lying on her side facing the window when he did return.

'I put the blanket back,' she said without turning. 'For one thing, I think I'm probably going to be cold without it, and for another it all seems rather pointless under the circumstances.' She was surprised by the steadiness of her voice. 'Anyway, you wouldn't get a wink of sleep in that chair.'

It seemed an age before a reply came. 'Probably not,' he agreed. 'It's pretty draughty out here with that wind howling round the eaves the way it is, I have to admit.'

He paused, then made a sudden decisive movement. 'In fact, I'm too chilled through to argue about it. Leo should have central heating in this place!'

'He doesn't need it,' said Dana. 'They don't use the place after October, remember.' Her body was tensed, waiting for the moment when the covers would be lifted, the mattress depressed by his weight. When it came it was almost an anticlimax, because there was scarcely any sag. For Leo nothing but the best would be good enough, she found herself thinking irrelevantly, even when it came to mattresses in a weekend cottage. At least she would have no difficulty staying on her own side. 'Goodnight,' she added.

'Goodnight.' Mark reached out a hand and switched off his bedside light, relaxing into the pillows with a faint sigh. 'With any luck the weather will have improved by morning.'

If it did it would be the only thing, Dana reflected, lying there in the darkness listening to the sound of the wind and rain on the windows. This was the first time in her life that she had ever shared a bed with anyone, yet it felt little different. Mark was staying strictly to his own side, responding to the invisible line drawn down the middle. They might well have been a dozen yards apart for all it meant.

It was still dark when she awoke, jerked from the depths of slumber by the weight of the arm thrown over her waist. Mark had moved the full width of the bed to lie beside her, body turned on one side, breath warm on her cheek. Only as she listened to his breathing did she realise he was still asleep and probably unaware of his actions, which very fact suggested that this was not the first time he had slept in such a position. Marion Gissard? she wondered painfully. Was she the one? How many times had Mark made love to her?

As if in direct response to her thoughts, the arm about her moved, the hand sliding upwards to find her breast and encircle it possessively. Dana froze to the touch, then as suddenly thawed, reacting instinctively to the warmth and feel of those lean fingers through the thin material of her nightgown, coming alive to other awakening senses in her body.

His name came to her lips on a whisper, drawn from some place deep down inside the contracting muscles of her stomach. Involuntarily she moved closer to him, feeling the hard length of his thigh against hers, the brush of his hair at her temple. Her own touch was tentative, feathering lightly across the hair of his chest and down over one bare, muscular shoulder to follow his arm back up to the hand which held her.

He said something indistinctly, and rolled over, coming on top of her as he found her mouth in a kiss that had nothing of tentativeness about it. Dana responded to it blindly, aware of his arousal and needing to know more—yearning to know it all.

The lift of his head was abrupt, his whole body tensed to sudden realisation. For a brief moment he remained where he was gazing down at her in the darkness, then with a muffled oath he slid away from her, flinging back the bedclothes to come to a sitting position on the edge of the bed with his back turned to her.

'Why didn't you waken me?' he demanded roughly. 'You must have realised . . .'

'That you thought I was someone else?' she finished for him as he broke off. Her voice sounded very small and tremulous. 'So what if I did? At least I was being treated like a woman.'

'You're not a woman,' he said between his teeth. 'That's the whole point!'

'I never shall be if someone doesn't make me one.' Dana came up on one elbow, body trembling to the emotions still running riot inside her. 'Mark, it doesn't matter that you don't love me. I know a man doesn't have to be in love to make love. You wanted me just now—you can't deny that much.'

'I wanted a simple physical satisfaction,' he came back on a hard note. 'Right then you were just a warm, available body, and that's all.'

'I don't believe you.' The tremor was still there despite all she could do to eradicate it. 'You might have thought I was someone else in your mind, but it was me you were reacting to physically.'

It was a moment before he answered that one, and when he did it was with force. 'I am not making love to you to satisfy girlish curiosity!'

'Then I'll find someone else who will!' she flashed back, losing the tremor in sudden searing anger and hurt.

Mark's lunge across the bed to grab her by the arm was too swift and fierce to be avoided. She gave a small cry of pain as he dragged her bodily towards him, seeing the glitter in his eyes with a sense of apprehension. Then as abruptly as he had seized her, he let her go, visibly regaining control of himself as he watched her rub at her bruised flesh.

'You very nearly got what you're asking for,' he said on a low note. 'Do you want me to hurt you, Dana?'

She shook her head numbly, unable to look him in the eye. 'All I want is for you to stop treating me like a schoolgirl. If a perfect stranger can guess things aren't as they should be between us, how long do you think it's going to take your father to suspect the same?'

'What are you talking about?'

'I overheard Cathy and Ian talking downstairs. She thinks there's something odd about our marriage.'

'You mean you deliberately listened.'

'All right, so I listened.' She refused to be defensive about it. 'I thought I was entitled, seeing it was us they were discussing.' She made herself look at him then. 'You were the one who didn't want any hint of anything unusual to get back to Julian.'

'Occupying separate rooms is a rather different matter from a vague notion,' Mark responded. 'Anyway, that's a chance I'll have to take. As to my father . . . well, he's hardly likely to suspect anything unless you give him good reason.'

'Don't worry, I shan't.' Her tone was subdued. 'For his sake I'll even pretend to be deliriously happy.'

He said on a softer note, 'Dana, you're seventeen. You've years yet to find the right man to make you that.'

'Providing I can find one who wants a wife with one failed marriage already behind her.'

'By then you'll be free to explain the circumstances.' Mark was holding on to his patience with an obvious effort. 'I've no intention of claiming marital privileges, so to all intents and purposes you'll be starting from square one once the annulment goes through. Now, go on back to sleep.'

'There doesn't have to be an annulment.' She was desperate to find some means of convincing him. 'I can learn to be the kind of wife you need—in every way.' Without allowing herself time to consider, she knelt up on the mattress and slid her arms about his neck, putting her lips to his with almost feverish intensity. 'I'm not too young for you, Mark. I'm not! Anything Marion Gissard can do I can do too. All you have to do is teach me!'

For a fleeting moment he did nothing, sitting there like a statue, his whole body rigidly held. When he did make a move it was roughly, his hands lifting to seize her wrists and forcibly peel them away from him, pushing her back on to the pillows.

'There's no way I'm going to teach you anything,' he

stated grimly. 'Just get that through your head. And leave Marion Gissard out of it too! You don't know anything about her.'

'I'm sure *you* know everything!' Pride put the words into her mouth. 'You should have married her when you had the chance, then this couldn't have happened.'

'That's enough. In fact, that's more than enough.' He sounded like a man fast approaching the end of his tether. 'You'd better get right back between those sheets.'

Dana obeyed because there was little point in doing anything else. She felt tense and miserable and bitterly ashamed of the impulse which had caused her to throw herself at his head the way she had. Mark didn't want her at any price. He had made that abundantly clear. She had to accept it. Only it wasn't going to be easy, because the ache was still there, lingering deep and immovable.

Mark put a pillow lengthways down the bed between the two of them before lying down again himself.

'That should stop any further wanderings on my part,' he said with self-directed irony. 'At least the wind seems to have died down, so our guests shouldn't have any difficulty in getting back to the mainland.'

Dana made no answer. There seemed nothing to say. She wished she could leave with them. Even Aunt Eleanor's was preferable to this.

She must have slept eventually, for when she next opened her eyes it was daylight. Mark was still dead to the world, one arm flung across his eyes as if to shield them from any intruding light, his jaw dark with bristle. She slid from the bed very slowly and carefully so as not to rouse him, and gathered together the clothing she needed, hoping the bathroom would not be in use. She wanted to be fully dressed and in command of herself before she saw anyone this morning.

There was no sound from the other room. Dana took a quick shower and got into the jeans and sweater she had brought with her, tying her hair back into a knot at her nape. Her face in the mirror looked surprisingly normal. But then why should it look otherwise? she asked herself. Nothing had happened to make her any different on the outside.

Ian was already in the kitchen when she got downstairs. He was dressed in his own clothes, and had coffee made.

'I've been up about an hour,' he confessed when she expressed surprise on seeing him. 'Couldn't get back to sleep. Nothing to do with the bed,' he added hastily. 'It's very comfortable. Cathy never stirred.' He watched her pour herself a cup of coffee from the pot, his whole demeanour one of discomfiture. 'I know I keep saying it,' he got out at length, 'but I really do feel bad about landing on you like this. Especially as we're not even— well, you know. It was very broad-minded of your husband to offer us a room together, considering.'

'Mark is thirty-five,' Dana said. 'That hardly makes him one of the Victorian generation. I don't suppose he saw much sense in splitting the two of you up when all you had to do was wait until we were asleep to get together again.'

'I suppose you're right.' His eyes were on her face, diffidence giving way to curiosity without too much of a struggle. 'There's a big age difference between you, isn't there?'

'Yes.' She saw no reason to tell him just how big. She couldn't meet his gaze full on, too uncertain of her ability to conceal inner feelings. 'I'm glad the gale didn't last too long. Do you think you'll get a ferry across all right this morning?'

'Oh yes. No trouble at all.' If he realised she was deliberately changing the subject he gave no sign of it. I've got to get the car down to a garage first, of course.

That means one journey to fetch enough to get her started.'

'I'll run you down after breakfast,' said Mark, coming into the kitchen on the last few words. 'We'll have to borrow a can.'

Dana moved towards the cooker without looking at him, aware that he must have got up almost immediately after she had left the room. Had he been awake all the time? she wondered. If so, why had he pretended? She wouldn't be asking him, she knew that. She wouldn't be asking him anything ever again.

Cathy came down some ten minutes later, wrinkling her nose pleasurably to the smell of grilling bacon.

'That's worth getting up for,' she said. She made no offer to help, sliding out a chair from the table and sinking into it to reach for the coffee pot. 'Anyone know what time the gale blew itself out?'

It was Mark who answered her from his seat on the other side of the table. 'Some time after midnight. We were lucky. It could have gone on for days.'

'And you'd have been stuck with us,' she came back cheerfully. 'Oh well, we'll be out of your hair before long.'

Leaving her alone again with Mark, Dana thought, eyes fixed on the eggs sizzling in the pan. At least she would have her own room back. She couldn't have taken another night of sharing.

The two men left soon after they finished eating, leaving Cathy to be picked up by Ian who would have to pass the end of the lane on his way to the garage again.

'How long do you plan on staying?' asked the former, stirring herself to bring the plates across to the sink where Dana was running hot water. 'It's not exactly honeymoon weather, is it?'

'We're leaving on Saturday,' Dana admitted. 'Mark

has to be back in town next week.'

'Business calls, and all that?' The tone was light. 'My father's in banking. Not in the same sense, of course. He only made manager of the local branch.' She paused. 'How did you two meet?'

Dana squirted washing-up liquid into the bowl and made suds with her hands. 'My father is a client of Mark's,' she said with truth.

'Oh?' This time the pause was longer. 'Are you in love with him?'

Dana stiffened involuntarily, her hands stilled in their movements. 'Of course,' she said swiftly—too swiftly. 'What kind of a question is that?'

'A personal one.' The other girl sounded quite unapologetic about it. 'I'm what's commonly known as a nosey parker. You've got to admit, it's not all that usual for a man his age to marry a girl yours. Not that he comes across the way you might expect somebody like that to do.'

Dana forced herself to continue with the dishes. 'You mean you were waiting for him to try separating you two last night?'

'Something like that, I suppose. Especially when it meant he had to come and share with you whether you wanted it or not.'

This time Dana gave up all pretence, standing there like a graven image with her eyes closed. 'How did you know?' she got out.

'The bed had been slept in,' came the calm response. 'Not that we minded that a bit. In fact, I only realised because the bottom sheet hadn't been straightened. Typical of a man making a bed. They'll only bother with the bit that shows.'

How on earth had changing the sheets slipped her mind? Dana wondered numbly. Why hadn't Mark thought of it too, if it came to that? She knew why, of course. The whole thing had been done in such a rush.

Quite unnecessarily, as it had turned out. Cathy was fully in the picture.

'Look, don't get upset,' advised the older girl comfortingly. 'I was scared myself the first time. I mean—well, it's different for them—they don't have to go through what we have to go through. Just tell yourself it's only once and it will soon be over. After that it's fantastic, just wait and see!'

'Don't!' Dana's whole face felt on fire. 'Please stop talking about it like that!'

'Why? There's nothing wrong in being open about things. I'll bet that husband of yours would be the first to agree you need somebody to talk to. No wonder he looks a bit grim sometimes—I mean, it can't be much of a picnic for him either.'

Dana took a towel and roughly dried her hands, her teeth clenched against the need to say what was in her mind. 'I'm going upstairs,' she said instead. 'Don't bother with the rest of the dishes. I'll finish them myself later.'

Cathy's shrug bespoke tolerant resignation. 'It's your funeral.'

The bedroom was cold compared with the warmth downstairs, but Dana barely noticed. Sitting on the bed, she thought back over the last few minutes and wondered what Cathy would have said if she only knew the truth of the matter. Afraid of Mark's lovemaking; that was almost funny! She could still feel the touch of his hands on her body, the ache deep inside. If he would only give her the chance she could make him forget the years between them, she knew she could.

By the time the cars came up the lane she was frozen to the marrow. Although she got to her feet she couldn't bring herself to go down and say goodbye to the two of them, terrified that Cathy would take it into her head to say something in front of Mark. Half expecting the latter to fetch her, she was relieved moments later to hear the

MG pull away. What she was going to tell Mark she had no idea, but at least there would be no listening ears.

She found him in the sitting room when she did go down, seated in front of a blazing fire. Dana went over and crouched in front of it, stretching her hands to the flames.

'This place really isn't designed for winter living,' she said.

There was a pause before Mark answered, as if he were waiting for her to add something else to the bare statement. 'I was going to give you five more minutes,' he said, 'and then come and find you. What happened?'

Denying that anything had was obviously futile. 'Cathy got a little too inquisitive,' she admitted.

'About what?'

'Us.' She tried to keep her tone expressionless. 'We forgot to change the sheets in your room. Cathy noticed, and drew her own conclusions.'

'Which were?' His own voice was quite unemotional.

There was no way round it. It had to be said. Dana gazed fixedly at the flames. 'She thinks I'm scared of the physical side of marriage and wouldn't let you sleep with me on our wedding night. She seems to have got quite a kick out of putting us in a position where we had to share a bed.'

'So that was what the innuendo was about.' He sounded suddenly grim. 'I'd try the "gentle touch" on her if I had her back here!' He paused, studying her. 'What did you tell her?'

'Nothing. That's why I went upstairs. We'll just have to hope she and Ian have the decency to keep our marital problems to themselves, that's all.'

'Yes.' The pause was longer this time. When he spoke again it was on a different note. 'Dana, last night . . .'

'I know,' she said levelly. 'It was all a mistake. If

you'd made love to me before you realised that I wasn't who you thought I was what would you have done then?'

'There's no way I could *not* have realised,' he said harshly.

'Why?' She made herself turn her head to look at him, her hurt in her eyes. 'Because I didn't respond the way an experienced woman might? That's hardly surprising, considering you keep denying me the experience.'

'And shall keep right on doing it.' His jaw was set. 'There's more to a relationship between a man and a woman then sexual intimacy. Compatibility means a great deal. You've missed out on too much, Dana. You need to travel, to mix with people, to have some light-hearted fun.'

'You're generalising,' she said huskily. 'Not all teen-agers are the same. We share a lot of the same tastes in things. Music, for instance. Or did you think I was only pretending to enjoy those concerts you took me to?'

Mark shook his head, the gesture weary. 'No, I didn't think you were pretending. You've a surprisingly well developed ear. It isn't just a case of liking the same things, it's being on the same wavelength.'

'The way you are with Marion Gissard?' Dana ignored the compression about his mouth, voice low and heavy. 'If this hadn't happened would you have married her eventually?'

The reply was a moment in coming, his expression once more under control. 'It's possible,' he admitted. 'We've known one another a long time.'

'I see.' Dana got stiffly to her feet. 'I'll go and move your things back to the other room.'

'Don't bother.' He sounded decisive. 'The mistake was in coming here in the first place. We won't compound it by staying any longer.'

She gazed at him numbly. 'We're going back to London?'

'No,' he said. 'We're going to move across to the mainland and book into a nice big impersonal hotel for a couple of nights. I'm having the spare bedroom at the apartment redecorated. It won't be ready before the weekend. Go and pack—there's an afternoon boat we can take.'

Dana went without argument, hardly caring whether they went or stayed. By his own admission Mark had been considering marrying Marion Gissard, and now here he was stuck with her instead. It explained so much about his attitude, and left little hope for any change.

CHAPTER SIX

IT was late Sunday evening before they finally returned to town. Dana was too tired to do more than take a cursory look about the room which was to be hers for at least the coming six months. Decorated in feminine blues and creams, it was, she supposed, a room with which any girl would be delighted. Any girl except herself. To her it was more like a prison cell; one in which she would no doubt be expected to spend a great deal of her time during the months ahead.

The last few days had not been all bad though, she reflected when she was in bed with the lights out, waiting for sleep to claim her. There had even been times when she and Mark had appeared to achieve some kind of rapport. If she could only teach her heart and her body to stop reacting to the very sight and sound of him, they might even attain that brother-and-sister relationship he had spoken of. What she needed was a diversion. Something to occupy her mind. There had to be something she could do, even if it were only volunteer visiting at one of the local hospitals. Perhaps that would teach her just how well off she really was. At least she had her health.

She awoke at nine to the sound of a vacuum cleaner and the realisation that Mark was in all probability already gone. By the time she was showered and dressed it was almost nine-thirty. Feeling more than a little ashamed of her tardiness, she went to find herself some breakfast.

Mrs Powell was in the kitchen with coffee already made. Dana had met her twice before, and found her rather awe-inspiringly efficient but not unfriendly. She was in her early fifties,and a widow with no children of her own, that much she knew. Coming here daily meant a journey of some fifty minutes each way, but Mark had said she preferred the independence of her own home. She didn't come in at weekends at all.

'I wasn't sure what you'd want to eat,' she said now as Dana hovered in the doorway, 'so I waited. There's plenty of eggs, and the bacon's only been in the fridge since Friday.'

'I only want toast, thanks,' said Dana. 'And I don't expect you to make it.' Put like that it sounded rather abrupt; she made haste to amend the statement. 'I mean, you have enough to do without waiting on me. I meant to be up earlier, but I just didn't wake up.'

'Won't do you any harm,' came the easy answer. 'Mr Senior said it was late when you got in last night.'

Dana looked at her quickly. 'You saw him this morning?'

'He was leaving as I arrived. It's usually the case. I've offered to cook him breakfast a hundred times or more, but he prefers to get it out at his club.'

Dana said nothing to that, but made a mental note to be up and around in good time the following morning. No matter what the circumstances, a man couldn't eat breakfast at his club when he had a wife at home to prepare it for him. What was Joseph Senior going to think if he heard *that* story!

If it came to that, she found herself wondering, what did Mrs Powell think of the separate rooms? After all, it was hardly common practice in this day and age. She doubted if she would ever know. The woman did not strike her as the type to make her opinions on the habits of her employer known. She would accept it the way she had accepted the marriage itself, without a blink of an eyelid.

The problem of what to do with herself became of

paramount importance during the hours following. Offering to help Mrs Powell was no solution, because the housekeeper had made it clear that she preferred to do the jobs herself. Probably because she knew that way they got done properly, Dana acknowledged with a wry little smile to herself. Certainly polishing furniture and washing down bathrooms held little real appeal.

It was around noon when her father rang. Hearing his voice on the phone after all that had happened gave her a strange sense of unreality.

'I thought I might catch you while I've got a few minutes to spare myself,' he said. 'How are things?'

Dana had taken the call in her room. Holding the receiver numbly to her ear, she tried to visualise the man at the other end of the line and found she couldn't. Pride came to her rescue, lending her voice a crispness of delivery she could never have achieved without it.

'Remarkably well considering. Am I supposed to regard this call as a further example of fatherly concern?'

The silence which greeted that remark was prolonged. When he came on again he sounded subdued. 'So he told you.'

'Yes, he told me,' she said. 'Wasn't it you yourself who called him an honourable man?'

'I shouldn't have thought him a stupid one,' he said. 'The fewer people who know about his brother, the better.'

'I'm hardly likely to threaten to go to the Press with the story,' Dana responded stiffly. 'I leave that kind of thing to you.' She closed her mind to the memory of her own bit of blackmail. That had been different anyway. She wouldn't have gone through with it. 'Even allowing for the fact that you were desperate for that loan extension, why bring me into it?'

'It seemed too good an opportunity to miss,' he

admitted. 'It was better than going back to Eleanor's, wasn't it?'

This time it was her turn to be silent for a moment or two. 'Do you mean,' she got out at last, 'that you were considering sending me back.'

'Well, you were hardly turning out to be the asset I thought you might be, were you?' His tone held a deliberate cruelty. 'I provided you with the rich kind of husband you certainly weren't going to get for yourself—any time. It's up to you what you make of it.'

'I'm sorry I was such a disappointment.' Dana had known it, yet the words still hurt. 'Perhaps you expected too much.'

'The way I did from your mother. You're like her in so many ways.'

'I'm glad!' She said it fiercely. 'I'm glad I'm like her and not like you! You know the main reason why Mark went through with the marriage? It was to get me away from your influence. So don't expect any kind of future help from your son-in-law, will you? He doesn't want to know.' She drew in a steadying breath, fighting for the control to see this through. 'That goes for me too.'

'I should have had a son.' There was bitterness in the statement. 'If that's the way you want it, Dana, it's fine by me. I shan't be ringing you again.'

Dana put down the receiver with fingers that trembled. Now that it was done she wanted to call him back. He was her father, after all, her kith and kin. Blood had to mean something, didn't it? She owed him some kind of loyalty if only because of that.

The answer came clear and sharp. She owed him nothing. Anything he had done for her had been to his own ends. Would anyone ever really love her, she wondered painfully, or was she destined to spend her life waiting in vain?

Life settled into a routine of sorts over the following days. True to her word, Dana made a point of getting up early each morning to cook breakfast for Mark, but she doubted if he really appreciated the gesture. At his age certain habits had become ingrained, she suspected. In all probability even having someone else living in the apartment at all was something of a strain. It would have been different had they been man and wife in the real sense, of course. Love would have carried them through.

The days dragged, despite all she could do to alleviate boredom. She knew no one in London, and Beverley was back at Leavybrook working towards her 'A' levels. Dana wished now that she had stayed on herself. There was very little chance that she would have gained any pass grades at all considering her 'O' level marks, but at least she would have been saved from this situation. She had always had trouble with any kind of examination, although her intelligence level was supposedly on a par with others in her year, and the suggestion that she forgo the strain of another year's work to no purpose had at first been a welcome one. Looking back from her present position, she could accept that there was a lot of truth in the old saying about schooldays being the happiest days of one's life.

If the days were bad, the evenings were only marginally better. Together, Dana and Mark would eat the meal prepared by Mrs Powell before she left for the day and exchange a limited conversation, then Mark would invariably retire to his study with the plea of work to be done, leaving her to amuse herself as best she could. His offer to provide a television for her entertainment she turned down flat, saying she would rather read. Watching flitting figures on a screen every night was no answer to her problem. What she needed was the reality of one solid figure.

'Tell Mrs Powell we shan't be needing dinner tonight,' he said on the Friday morning as he was getting into his overcoat. 'We're eating at the house.' The eyes meeting

Dana's were steady in their regard. 'It had to come sooner or later. Don't worry about it. All you have to do is act naturally.'

Which was easier said than done, Dana reflected when he had gone. Last time she had faced Joseph Senior she had believed herself secure in the knowledge of Mark's feelings for her. Shorn of that security, she doubted herself capable of dissembling enough to convince a sharp-eyed and shrewd man that all was well with his son's marriage, especially when he would be looking for even the faintest sign of incompatibility between her and Mark. But it had to be gone through; Mark was right about that. She would just have to do the best she could and hope that it was good enough.

She dressed carefully for the occasion, when the time arrived, choosing a classically plain little dress in dark green silk jersey, and stepping into her highest pair of heels. With her hair scooped up away from her face, she noted for the first time the hollows under her cheek-bones. She had lost weight this last week, she knew, but she hadn't realised how much it showed. The girlish roundness had vanished completely.

The house was as she remembered it: big and old, with a lot of wood panelling and fine furnishings. A maid took their things at the door, greeting Mark with the familiarity of long service with the family.

Mr Senior was in the library, she said, along with Mr Brendon. Dana stole a swift glance at Mark's face on hearing the lattter information, but gleaned nothing from his expression. For herself it was just one more bridge to cross.

She was disturbed by the deterioration in the banker since she had last seen him just ten days ago. His eyes were shrunken in their sockets, his skin bearing a greyish tinge. He greeted the pair of them without fuss, leaving it to Brendon to supply them with drinks and carry the bulk of the conversation, yet Dana could sense his watchfulness. She made every attempt to act the way a happy young bride might appear, determined to let nothing upset this man she barely knew but felt such compassion towards. To die was bad enough; to know one was dying and yet be unable to do anything about it infinitely worse.

She had Brendon by her side at dinner, while Mark sat opposite on his father's other hand. What the two of them talked about she had little idea, as most of her own attention was taken by her brother-in-law. Brendon could be the most entertaining of companions, she discovered when he set himself out to be. What he told her about Hawaii made her long to go there and see for herself.

'Are you really sure about not going back?' she asked at one point. 'You seem to have enjoyed life so much while you were out there.'

'Anything palls in time,' he rejoined lightly. 'Let's say I exhausted the possibilities. Mark can either appoint this man I put in as permanent manager when he goes out after Christmas, or alternatively find someone else.' He studied her for a moment, an odd expression in his eyes. 'You are both going, I take it?'

'Of course.' She said it without undue emphasis. 'I'm looking forward to it.'

'It's a honeymooners' paradise.' His voice was lazy. 'You can hardly count what you've already had as that, can you?'

In the momentary pause, Dana was aware that Mark and his father had stopped talking and were listening to the exchange—waiting for her reply. She made it with a smile she could only hope and trust did not look as forced as it felt. 'It doesn't really matter where, or for how long.'

'Just so long as the two of you are together,' he supplied. Very briefly his eyes sought those of his brother across the table, the blueness darkening. 'That's the essence of it, isn't it?'

'Providing the two are right for one another.' Mark's tone was quiet. 'Have you decided what you're going to do with yourself from here on in?'

The younger man shrugged. 'I've one or two ideas. Nothing concrete as yet. There's no great hurry, is there?'

'No, not at all. Just that when the time comes I might be able to put you in touch with the right people.'

'Thanks.' The smile had a slant to it. 'I'll remember that.'

It was later in the car heading back to the apartment that Dana ventured the question she had wanted to ask before. 'Was Brendon the reason you moved out and found a place of your own?'

'Part of it,' Mark admitted. 'We were never the kind of friends brothers perhaps should be. There was also the feeling that at thirty it was time I had a place of my own.'

'So it was five years ago not three,' she said unthinkingly, and drew a swift glance.

'Why would you think it might be three?'

'Something Brendon said at the wedding.' Having come this far it was impossible not to carry on. 'He told me that three years ago he was on the verge of getting married himself until . . .' she paused, searching for some way to put it . . . 'until someone else stepped in. He didn't mention you by name, but it was obvious who he meant.'

Mark didn't reply immediately. Lit by the yellow glow of the passing street lamps, his face looked austere. 'I suppose he had to see it that way,' he said at length. 'Anything would be better than simply accepting the fact that she didn't feel enough for him to marry him.'

Dana's voice was soft. 'Then you didn't deliberately take her away from him?'

'No, because he'd already lost her.'

'But you didn't marry her either.'

This time the pause was longer and somehow infused with meaning. Dana was on the very point of realisation when he finally put it into words.

'I told you I was considering it. I had been for some time. We were two very independent people, and I had to be sure I could accept a career woman as a wife.'

'And could you?' Her throat felt tight as a drum.

Mark's shrug was more sensed than seen. 'It's immaterial now.'

She made herself say it. 'It won't always be if you really intend having our marriage annulled. If you told her the truth she'd surely wait until February.'

'Who said anything about February?' he demanded. 'Do you really think I'm going to leave you to your own devices at eighteen? It's going to be a couple of years before you're anywhere near ready to look after yourself. That's when we'll start talking about annulments.'

'Unless I take it on myself to walk out first,' she rejoined huskily. 'You couldn't stop me, Mark. You might have some jurisdiction now because I'm still legally a minor, but once I'm of age I'm entirely my own person!'

'Living on what?'

Her chin lifted. 'I can get a job.'

'One that will pay enough to keep you, do you think?' He shook his head impatiently. 'You're talking nonsense, Dana. I've no intention of letting you walk out on me.'

It was useless arguing with him. He didn't believe she had the courage to carry out her threat. Come February, if she lasted that long, he was going to discover how wrong he was, she promised herself. Marion had more claim on him than she did.

The weekend was better than she had anticipated. Mark had theatre tickets for the Saturday evening, and afterwards took her to supper at a small but obviously exclusive restaurant just around the corner. There was no dancing, she noted, and wondered if he had chosen the place for that reason. He avoided contact with her wherever possible; she had noted that too. She tried to teach herself not to care, but there was no denying the pain it caused her.

Advertising in the morning papers gave Dana a jolt in the realisation that Christmas was less than two weeks away. She supposed she should get Mark something for the occasion. Certainly the monthly allowance he had placed to her account was more than adequate. So far she had spent nothing on herself because there was nothing she had needed. When the time came that such a step became necessary, she wasn't at all sure how she was going to feel about spending what her mind refused to accept as her own money. If she bought Mark a Christmas present it would be as though he had paid for it himself, she thought disconsolately. If only there were some way of earning herself a few pounds!

A possible solution came to her on the Monday while listening to a local radio summary of the Oxford Street scene as the countdown of shopping days got into its stride. Most of the larger stores took on extra staff for the pre-Christmas rush. Perhaps she could secure herself a temporary position of that nature.

And how would Mark be likely to react? came the immediate question, bringing a sudden sense of deflation. Not with approval, that was almost certain. He would consider her reasons totally inadequate. Yet did he really have to know, if it came right down to it? He was never home before six-thirty. Providing the hours were right she could be back here long before him. Ten till four would suit her.

'Going out?' asked Mrs Powell when she emerged from her room dressed in her most sensible skirt and jacket. 'You'll find it chilly without a topcoat.'

Dana thought she was probably right, but was also

aware that the only topcoat she possessed in addition to
the mink hardly suited the image she was trying to put
across.

'I'll be using taxis,' she said, doing a quick mental
calculation of her available resources, 'so I'm hardly
going to need it. I shan't be back for lunch.'

The taxi across town cost rather more than she had
bargained for, but Selfridges had seemed a good place
to start. She could have telephoned first to find out what
the possibilities were, she realised when it was too late,
and could have kicked herself for not thinking of it
sooner. The closer she got to her destination, the more
her enthusiasm had waned. She wasn't even sure who
she had to see to enquire about a job at all—the per-
sonnel officer, she imagined. She had to force herself to
enter the store.

Certainly there had been no exaggeration on the part
of the radio commentator. There were crowds both outside and in, the activity around every counter frenetic.
Caught up in the general surge of bodies, Dana moved
with the tide towards the escalators. Staff offices were
generally on the upper floor anyway. She would find
them sooner or later. Whether, having found them, she
pursued her original intention remained open to speculation. Right now she was content to let matters take
their own course.

She ran into Brendon quite literally in the toy department where he had stopped to watch a demonstration
of electronic games.

'These things fascinate me,' he admitted cheerfully,
revealing little surprise at the chance encounter. 'If
you're thinking of buying your favourite brother-in-law
a Christmas present, I'd settle quite happily for Space
Invaders.'

'You're supposed to accept with gratitude anything
offered,' Dana responded on a suitably light note,
unable to decide whether she was glad or sorry to see

him. For a fleeting moment she had thought he was Mark and been conscious of the sudden flood of guilty panic, regardless of the fact that she had not, so far, carried through her plan. And probably never would, she acknowledged now with a sense of resignation. It had been a ridiculous idea anyhow. 'I gather you're Christmas shopping too,' she added to underline her own change of heart. 'Hectic, isn't it?'

'It's all these foreigners,' he said, giving ground to a party of what sounded like Germans intent on reaching the pile of coloured boxes behind him. 'Look, it's gone twelve. Why don't we go and grab some lunch? I know a great little place not too far away where we'll get a table.'

Dana thought briefly of the apartment with only Mrs Powell for company and felt no desire to refuse the invitation. She had intended eating out in any case.

'That sounds a good idea,' she said. 'If we can ever get out of here again, that is.'

'Hold on to my hand,' Brendon advised, offering it. 'Then we shan't get separated. When it comes to forging paths I've no equal!'

Laughing, Dana allowed herself to be led through the milling throng, tethered by the firm grasp of his fingers. It was nice to be taken over like this, especially as she had anticipated a lonely meal. Unlike his brother, Brendon had time for her. It made a pleasant change.

The little place turned out to be a good ten minutes' walk away. By the time they reached it, Dana was chilled through by the cutting wind.

'I'd have taken a taxi if there'd been one available,' Brendon said ruefully when they were seated at a table and she was beginning to thaw out again. 'It always was just about impossible to find one this time of day.'

'It's all right,' she assured him. 'I'm fine now. It was my own fault for not wearing something warmer in the first place.'

'Yes, you're hardly dressed for December,' he agreed, eyeing the light wool jacket. 'In fact, to be blunt about it, you're hardly dressed the way I'd expect Mark's wife to be dressed at all—or has he changed so much in three years?'

Her smile was strained. 'If you mean does he care about the way I look, I'm not really sure. He never says anything.'

'Remiss of him. On Friday night you looked good enough to eat. Today . . .' he paused, studying her, head on one side and a question in his eyes . . . 'I'd say you were deliberately trying to look not too well off, if that didn't sound ridiculous.' He was watching her too closely to miss the reaction she could not control, his brows lifting a fraction. '*Is* it so ridiculous?'

'I had this idea about finding a temporary job,' she confessed after a moment. 'You see, I don't have any money of my own and . . .'

'You mean Mark doesn't make you an allowance?'

'Yes, of course he does. Only that's really his, and I wanted to get him a present he hadn't in effect paid for.' She spread her hands with a wry little shrug. 'Silly, wasn't it?'

'No.' His tone was soft. 'As a matter of fact, I think it's sweet. You know, you're a very unusual girl, Dana.'

'The word,' she said, 'is naïve.' She laughed. 'I was thinking I'd be able to keep it a secret from Mark. I never even considered the weekends, and Saturdays would be one of the main times extra sales staff were needed, wouldn't it? Anyway, I've given up the whole idea now.'

'So that's why you were wandering through Selfridges. When I saw you in the kids' department I thought maybe . . .' He stopped and shook his head . . . 'No, I guess not.'

'Thought what?' Dana insisted, then felt the colour come into her cheeks as realisation dawned. 'I'd hardly be looking at electronic games even if it were true,' she said on as light a note as she could manage. 'Anyway, we've only been married two weeks.' She met the blue eyes and felt her colour deepen even further. 'Oh,' she said. 'I see.'

'I'm probably not the only one who's considered that angle,' he defended. 'With that much difference in your ages, it seemed a reasonable assumption. The only part I found difficult to accept was that Mark would put himself in such a position in the first place. Whatever else he may be, he's no fool.' The pause held deliberation. 'Which brings me to the question of why he actually did marry you.'

Dana lifted her chin. 'What makes you so sure it wasn't for the normal reasons?'

'Because of the way he treats you. He's more like a guardian than a husband.'

The arrival of a waiter to take their order saved Dana from finding an immediate reply, but she knew she was not off the hook by any means. Brendon had more perception than she would have given him credit for—more probably than many people gave him credit for. And tenacity too; she could see that in his eyes. He wasn't going to let this drop easily.

She was proved right in her assessment the moment the waiter departed when he came right back into the attack.

'There's something about this whole business that doesn't jell,' he said. 'Are you going to tell me, or do I start guessing?'

'I . . . can't.' Her voice came out low and unsteady.

'All right, so I'll guess.' His own tone was muted, confining the conversation to their own table. 'He lost his head over you once and felt responsible. Now that I can imagine, at a pinch.'

'It wasn't like that,' she responded desperately. 'Brendon, please let's talk about something else.'

'No way.' He was gentle but adamant. 'You're going to tell me all about it, Dana. You want to, don't you? You need to get it off your chest.'

He was right, she had to admit. It would be such a relief to talk about it openly, to stop pretending. Brendon was Mark's brother; it wasn't like telling a stranger. He was entitled to know about Gary if nothing else.

It was difficult to know at which point to start, but once she did begin the words came without prompting, pouring from her like a stream overflowing its banks. She held nothing back, refusing to find excuses for her own over-eager acceptance of the situation.

'I suppose I wanted to be convinced,' she concluded ruefully. 'I was so bowled over that a man like Mark would even notice me.'

'Any man would notice you,' Brendon put in emphatically. 'That father of yours should be shot! Not that Mark doesn't have to take his share of the blame too. There had to be a better way round it than this.'

'Except that he started to feel responsible for me.' She paused, conscious of a sense of release from the strain of the past couple of weeks. She had someone to talk to at last; someone she could trust. Brendon was so much more approachable than his brother, so relaxing to be with. 'You don't seem very surprised about Gary,' she added.

'As a matter of fact, Mark already told me about him on Friday when Dad was showing you his coin collection. I agreed with him at the time about the wisdom in keeping it to ourselves. Now I'm not so sure.'

'You're not suggesting he should have let my father carry out his threat? A shock like that could have killed your father!'

'He's dying already.' Brendon spread his hands at the look on her face, tone wry. 'I know that sounds callous, but it's the plain, honest truth. Anyway, there's no guarantee that your father would have gone ahead. People say a lot of things they don't necessarily mean when they're in a fix.'

Dana shook her head. 'He meant it. I don't think he has a conscience. In any case, it's all rather immaterial now, isn't it? Mark's stuck with me.' She hesitated before saying it. 'At least it leaves Marion free again.'

'So you know about that too.' He smiled a little. 'Two years ago, or even a year ago, I might have felt tempted to chance my luck again. Now there isn't the least inclination. She made her choice.'

'You think it was a free one?'

'Not in the way you mean.' The smile was still there but edged with cynicism. 'Mark saw something he fancied for himself and made sure she realised he was the better prospect, that's all.'

Dana said quickly, 'But he didn't tell her he'd marry her, did he?'

'I've no idea what he told her. The first I knew was when she gave me back my ring and said she'd changed her mind. Within a month they were going everywhere together.'

'And that's when you decided to go to Hawaii?'

'It seemed a good idea at the time. Otherwise I might have finished up doing something that would have put even Gary's activities in the shade.' His glance went beyond her. 'Here comes our soup.'

He chattered lightly about the coming festive season

while the waiter busied himself with the dishes, returning to the former topic only when they were alone again. 'Tell me,' he said, 'how do you really feel about Mark now?'

'I'm not sure,' Dana admitted. 'I honestly thought I was in love with him, but now I'm beginning to wonder if he was right when he said it was only infatuation. You see, I've no one to ask.'

'You have me.' His tone lacked any element of banter. 'And I can tell you, if you loved him you wouldn't need to ask anyone's opinion. You'd know.'

'I suppose so.' Her heart felt heavy. 'I'm not sure whether that makes it better or worse.'

'Better, once you've got used to the idea, because it gives you a certain freedom.' He paused, eyed her consideringly for a moment then appeared to make up his mind. 'Under normal circumstances, I wouldn't have dreamed of telling you what I'm going to tell you, but it might even help. Mark is seeing Marion again.'

Dana stared at him, her soup forgotten. 'What does that mean exactly?' she got out at length.

'They were seen together last week. Early evening it was, having drinks in a hotel bar. It could be quite innocent, of course, but in that case he would surely have mentioned it. Was there an evening when he arrived home fairly late?'

'Yes.' Her voice seemed to be coming from a long distance away. 'Wednesday—it must have been around seven-thirty. He said he'd been seeing a client.'

'There you are, then. I'd say that gave you carte blanche.'

'To do what?'

'Start enjoying yourself, for one thing. I'm as free as the air myself for the next few weeks, if it's company you need.'

She said painfully, 'Is this your way of trying to get back at Mark for what he did to you?'

'No.' He sounded totally sincere. 'All I'm offering is friendship. Right now it's all you need. You've had a bad time, and I'd like to try making it up to you to some extent. If I don't advocate telling Mark about it, that's because I think he'd turn dog-in-the-manger about it. Expecting you to spend all day and every day mooching around on your own is a bit much, especially if . . .' he paused there and shrugged . . . 'well, it speaks for itself.'

'Especially if he's spending time with Marion,' she finished for him, twisting the screw a little deeper. 'I don't have any actual proof that he's doing that, though, do I? He's been seen once having a drink with her. All right, he didn't tell me about it, but that doesn't have to mean there was anything in it.'

'No?' Brendon asked quietly.

Dana bit her lip. 'So I'm being naïve again. Mark admitted he'd been considering asking her to marry him before all this happened. Perhaps he's decided that half a loaf is better than none.' She met his eyes bravely, forcing a faint smile. 'After all, two years living with a kid sister has to have certain drawbacks.'

'For most men,' Brendon agreed. 'So?'

'I'll think about it,' she promised. 'I really will. And thanks, Brendon. It's nice to know I have someone to talk to if I want to.'

'Any time at all.' He reached across and gently touched her cheek. 'You need your confidence building up again!'

'I never had too much to start with,' she confessed. 'I suppose that's partly why I wanted so much to believe Mark wanted me for myself.'

Brendon said gruffly, 'He's a fool that he doesn't. You won't always be seventeen.'

But the gap would always be there, thought Dana in

painful acceptance. She must have been mad to think eighteen years could ever be bridged. They were a whole world apart.

CHAPTER SEVEN

MARK came home unexpectedly early that evening, arriving before Mrs Powell had left for once.

'I'm afraid I have to go out again,' he said when Dana expressed her surprise. 'I've an appointment with Sir Edward Keen, the industrialist.' He paused as if in anticipation of some comment, a look of faint impatience crossing his features when none was forthcoming. 'These things can't always be confined to daytime hours.'

'You don't have to explain.' Her tone was creditably level. 'I understand perfectly. Are you having dinner out too?'

'No, I'll eat first—I'm not due until eight-thirty. Give me fifteen minutes to shower and change, then pour me a Scotch, will you?'

How to make the little woman feel indispensable, thought Dana with wry humour as he vanished in the direction of his own room. Pouring drinks was about the only thing he would allow her to do for him, and even that only when he happened to think of it. She wondered if he really was going to see Sir Edward as he said, or if that was simply a cover. After what Brendon had told her it was only natural she should feel suspicious, she defended herself. Not that she could blame Mark too much if he found himself unable to turn his back on Marion any longer. If their own relationship held little for her it held even less for him.

Perhaps things really would be better if they each lived their own lives, she reflected dully. Brendon's offer had been a genuine one, she was sure. He liked her and he

wanted to help. That was a comfort in itself. And yet
Mark wouldn't condone such a friendship, she was sure
of that too. If she accepted it would have to be without
his knowledge, and that step she wasn't quite ready to
take. Not without proof that he was seeing Marion on a
regular basis. Anyone could meet once by accident.
Today in Selfridges was proof of that. If he hadn't mentioned having a drink with Marion it was probably because he saw little point, just as she saw little point in
telling him about Brendon.

He looked very much the business-man still when he
came back to the drawing room, which fact alone reassured her a little. He took the glass she handed him,
and sank to a seat by the fireside with a sigh of satisfaction.

'This is the first time I've felt able to relax all day,' he
said. 'It's a busy time of year.' He took a swallow of the
whisky, eyes seeking her face as he brought the glass
down again. 'I rang through around two, and Mrs
Powell said you'd gone shopping. Buy anything
interesting?'

'I didn't buy anything,' Dana admitted. 'I was just
window-shopping . . . you know, looking for ideas.' If
ever there was a time for mentioning her meeting with
Brendon that time was now, but she didn't take advantage of the opportunity. 'What did you phone about?'
she added curiously.

'Oh, nothing in particular.' He took another pull at
the whisky, expression unrevealing. 'You don't get a lot
of entertainment out of life at present, I'm afraid. We'll
have to make up for it after Christmas when we go to
Maui.'

She said hesitantly, 'Do you think it's going to be a
good time to be away? Your father looked so drawn on
Friday night.'

'He isn't going to make Easter, that's for certain.'
The agreement was quiet but the faint compression

about his jawline told its own story. 'We'll wait and see how it goes.'

'Brendon said on Friday that the property had been in the family for a long time.' She kept her tone carefully neutral.

Mark nodded. 'My grandfather bought it to retire to. Dad planned on doing the same.'

It was the first time she had heard him use the affectionate diminutive. It underlined the quality of his regard more subtly than any other word could have done. 'And you?' she asked softly.

Some indefinable spark briefly lit the blue eyes. 'I have plans,' he said. 'They depend on a number of factors.'

They would have to, Dana reflected. Thirty years was a long time to plan ahead. She tried to think about where she might be in thirty years' time, failing because imagination didn't stretch that far. She would be old, for one thing—or middle-aged at least. She could only hope that by then she would have found some measure of fulfilment.

Mark left soon after they finished supper, telling her not to wait up as he was likely to be late. With the dishes stacked and the dishwasher switched on, Dana wandered restlessly about the drawing room, picking up an ornament here a book there and failing to take any real interest in either. Eventually, stirred by an impulse she didn't want to examine too closely, she went to the study, sitting down behind Mark's leather-topped desk with a sense of intrusion. There was little clutter, just a few neatly piled folders and a couple of reference books along with the silver pen tray. The telephone in here was on a different line, that much she knew. She hesitated only momentarily before reaching out to press the appropriate letter on the dial-a-page directory sited beneath the set.

There were several names and numbers listed under 'G', but not the one she sought. She found it under 'M'

for Marion, and sat there looking at it for several
moments while she fought a battle with her conscience.
Supposing the woman wasn't in, what would that prove?
Coincidences happened all the time. And if she was,
what was she going to say? If it came to that, how would
she know whether Mark was there or not?

No argument worked. Dialling the number with unsteady fingers, she thought it would serve her right if
Mark himself answered the call. The sound of the receiver being lifted at the other end brought a sensation
like falling through space as she waited for her fears to
be realised, but the voice when it came was unmistakably
female, complemented by the music audible in the background. Beethoven's Fifth, Dana realised. One of Mark's
favourite pieces; he had told her so himself. It still meant
nothing, of course. It could also be one of Marion's own.

'Hallo?' repeated the latter on a rising inflection. 'Is
anyone there?'

Dana put down the receiver without saying a word,
lacking the courage to risk recognition. She was no wiser
now, and hardly deserved to be. Even if Mark had
proved to be lying to her, what would she have done
about it? He owed her no fidelity as such.

She was in bed but not asleep when she heard him
come home. Her bedside clock said ten minutes after
midnight. Lying gazing numbly at the darkened ceiling,
she wondered if there would ever come a time when she
could accept the situation as it was. Brendon was right:
what she needed was something else to occupy her mind.
She would ring him tomorrow.

If her resolve had faltered a little by morning it was
strengthened again by Mark's announcement that he
had to make an overnight trip.

'It isn't something I can hand over to someone else,
unfortunately,' he said at breakfast. 'Are you going to
be all right here on your own, or shall we ask Mrs Powell
to stay through with you?'

'I think it might be a bit short notice for Mrs Powell,' Dana replied, trying not to let her feelings show. 'Anyway, I'm used to being on my own.'

'I know, and I'm sorry.' He sounded weary. 'Things will ease up soon, but until they do I'm afraid you're just going to have to put up with it. Don't you have any friends you can ring?'

Her eyes met his briefly and slid away again. 'I have one,' she said. 'I might do that.'

'Good.' His relief was patent. 'We'll drive down to Brighton on Sunday and have lunch in style, that's a promise.' He was draining his coffee cup even as he stood up. 'I'll see you tomorrow. Can't say what time, it depends when we get through.'

Dana waited until the outer door had opened and closed again before getting to her feet. Mrs Powell was late this morning. If she was going to ring Brendon at all it should be now, while there was no possibility of anyone overhearing. And ring him she must. She needed him. If Mark didn't like it if and when he found out, that was too bad. For once she was going to do what *she* wanted to do.

Betty, the maid, answered the phone. Dana gave her name without hesitation, telling herself there was nothing strange about a girl telephoning her brother-in-law. Brendon sounded truly delighted to hear her voice.

'I only just got up,' he said. 'Lazy beggar, that I am. To be honest, I didn't expect to hear from you so soon— if at all.' He paused, his very silence holding a question.

'Mark had to go away,' she said. 'He won't be back until tomorrow. I thought ...' She broke off there, barely knowing what she had thought.

'You'd like company,' he supplied for her. 'That's what I'm here for.' His tone briskened. 'Be down on the corner in one hour and I'll pick you up in a taxi.'

'Where are we going?' she asked, fighting the urge to back down and tell him she had changed her mind.

His laugh was infectious. 'For starters, we're going to find ourselves a willing kid and visit a Santa's Grotto or two, just to get us in the festive mood. After that we'll have lunch at McDonald's followed by, if I can manage to arrange it, a helicopter flight over central London. Sound good so far?'

'It sounds great!' Dana was laughing too, carried along on the wave of his enthusiasm. 'Isn't it going to cost rather a lot?'

'That's my concern. All you have to do is sit back and enjoy yourself. Tonight . . .' he paused again, voice taking on a different note . . . 'well, we'll talk about that later. One thing you're not going to be doing is sitting around that place twiddling your thumbs. An hour.'

Dana was unable to deny the surge of anticipation as she put down the receiver. Brendon was so different from his brother, so capable of creating a carefree mood. Never in a thousand years could she imagine Mark suggesting any of the things Brendon had just suggested, especially the McDonald's lunch. Not his fault, of course, she defended loyally. If Marion was an example of the kind of women he had grown accustomed to over the years, it was hardly surprising that he might take it for granted all her sex preferred the more sophisticated pursuits.

Mrs Powell arrived while she was dressing. She was polishing the lobby table when Dana emerged from her room warmly and comfortably dressed in cord slacks tucked into the tops of calf-length boots, and sheepskin jacket.

'Going out again?' asked the housekeeper mildly. 'What about lunch?'

'I shan't be in,' Dana told her, adding on impulse, 'We shan't be needing an evening meal either, so why not take the afternoon off? I'm sure you must have plenty of Christmas shopping to do.'

'Not so much,' came the response. 'There's only my

sister and me to think about these days. Still, it would give me an opportunity to have a browse through Harrods. It's too much trouble to come back into town Saturday mornings.' She smiled her rare smile. 'I'll take you up on that.'

Dana left the apartment feeling pleased with herself for having made the suggestion. Everyone deserved a break from routine occasionally. For the first time it occurred to her to wonder what Mark's plans for Christmas Day might be. Would he be expecting her to organise dinner, for instance? Had things been normal between them she could have imagined nothing better than a Christmas spent alone together, but under present circumstances the thought held little appeal. She would have to bring the matter up when he got back, she told herself, shaking off the threatening depression. For now, she was going to enjoy Brendon's company and forget about everything else.

The promised taxi was just drawing up as she reached the corner of the block. Brendon got out to greet her, putting her at ease immediately with his casual manner. He was dressed informally too, his leather jacket lined in fur and buttoned over a white rollnecked sweater, reminding Dana all too potently of the way Mark had looked at the cottage. She closed her mind to the invading image, determined to let nothing spoil this day. Mark hadn't cared about leaving her alone why should she care for his feelings?

Enjoy the day she did. They both did. Being with Brendon was more fun than Dana had ever experienced. She revelled in his attention, in his teasing, in his sheer assumption of familiarity. They were family, as he said. Why stand on ceremony?

'I should have had a brother,' she said wistfully in the taxi coming back from the heliport. 'Although I suppose he might have turned out to be like my father if I had.'

'Could be,' Brendon agreed. 'Firstborn sons usually

follow in father's footsteps.'

'But not second ones.' She stole a glance at him, heart
jerking to the cut of his profile. 'Is it really true you
never wanted to go into the bank?'

'Perfectly,' he said. 'Neither did Gary. I was in advertising when I met Marion. I might be again if a job
turns up. I'll start putting out feelers right after
Christmas.'

'Mark said he could put you in touch with the right
people,' Dana ventured. 'Won't you be taking him up
on it?'

He looked at her then, mouth tilted. 'Would you?'

'I don't suppose so,' she admitted after a moment.
'Not if I still held a grudge.' Her smile was over-bright.
'It's been a fabulous day, Brendon! I've loved every
minute!'

'It isn't over yet,' he said. 'I'm going to drop you off
and go home to change, then we're going to take in a
night club.'

'I don't think I can,' she said uncertainly, and saw his
jaw firm.

'Of course you can. What's to stop you?'

'I'm under age, for one thing.'

'If we don't tell them, they'll never guess. Wear your
hair up—that makes you look older.' He pressed his
knuckles under her chin, smiling at her expression.
'You're a big girl now. It's time you had a real night
out on the town. No one will know. It will be our
secret.'

She gave in because she wanted to; because she
couldn't resist the temptation. 'All right, I'll come. What
time?'

'Make it seven-thirty,' he said, 'then we can eat first.
The place I have in mind puts on a good floor show,
but isn't first class cuisine.' He paused, a curious expression in his eyes. 'Did you ever dance the night
away?'

'No,' she admitted, 'but I'm willing to try.'

'That's all it takes.' He switched his gaze to the window as the vehicle turned a corner. 'Here we are now, and it's barely five. Two and a half hours should be long enough, even for a woman.'

Dana laughed, relishing rather than resenting the generalisation. Tonight she would be a woman—all woman. She would make Brendon proud to be with her. Let Mark stay away as long as he liked. While she had his brother for company she didn't need him.

She was ready by seven in the low-cut black dress which had drawn Mark's disapproval that very first night, aware of defiance in the gesture. With half an hour to go before Brendon arrived to collect her, she tried to interest herself in a magazine, but soon gave it up. She knew what she wanted to do; she had known all along. The question was, why bother?

She was still asking herself that same question when she sat down at the study desk again, only it didn't seem to make any difference. She let the ringing tone go on for almost a minute before returning the instrument to its rest. Not conclusive, of course. Marion could be anywhere. All the same——

Brendon arrived promptly on the half hour to find her bright-eyed and sparkling.

'I see you started without me,' he commented in dry amusement, eyeing the sherry glass still in her hand. 'No, I won't have one, thanks. I kept the cab waiting.' He took up her coat, holding it out for her to slide in her arms, his hands lingering briefly on her shoulders. 'I like the dress, by the way.'

'Mark thinks it's too old for me,' she said without meaning to, and sensed his smile.

'*He's* too old for you,' he said. 'Anyway, we're going to forget Mark for tonight. Aren't we?'

'Willingly,' she agreed. She spun to face him, hands lifting the collar of the mink to frame her face, the sparkle deliberately emphasised. 'Let's go!'

The effects of that first sherry were beginning to wear off by the time they reached the restaurant where Brendon had booked a table, so she had another in the bar before going in. He ordered wine with the meal without consulting her, but she drank it anyway, feeling any remaining tension float away as her spirits soared.

'You know, I think you're better-looking than Mark,' she announced judiciously at one point, studying her companion across the table. 'I'm not sure why, because feature for feature you're so much alike, yet it's there. Perhaps it's because you smile more.'

'Perhaps I've more to smile about,' Brendon countered lightly. 'You do realise you're very close to being intoxicated, don't you?'

Dana laughed. 'I realise I'm having a wonderful time. When are we going on to this nightclub? I feel like dancing.'

'Just as soon as I've paid the bill here,' he said, and lifted a hand to summon the waiter.

The taxi ride to the club seemed to take only seconds. Looking out at the lights whisking by, Dana felt as if she were on a merry-go-round. She was glad to find her feet on solid ground once more, lifting her face to the cold night air and breathing in deeply as Brendon paid off the driver. That was better. She felt almost normal again. All the same, she welcomed the arm that came lightly about her as they moved into the club entrance.

Inside there was dimness and the smell of smoke. Someone relieved Dana of her coat before they went through to a larger room which had curtained stage at one end and tables around the perimeter. People were dancing in the cleared central space to the music provided by a four-piece combo housed in an alcove adjacent to the stage.

'It used to be a small theatre,' Brendon explained a little unnecessarily when they were seated at one of the rear tables raised slightly above the front rank by means of a platform. 'The first show doesn't start till ten-thirty, so we're in ample time.'

Dana was watching the dancers, gaze lingering on those few of the women present wearing long dresses. 'Are they hostesses?' she asked uncertainly, and heard his laugh.

'Yes, but don't let your imagination run away with you. They're here to dance with and provide companionship for any man without a partner of his own, but that's as far as it goes. The rules have to be strict or the licence gets revoked. Ah, here comes our champagne!'

A part of Dana's mind knew full well that she should refuse the sparkling glass put before her a moment or two later, but she ignored the message, laughing as the bubbles tickled her nose. Brendon was going all out to give her a night to remember. The least she could do was show her appreciation by enjoying every moment.

'I'm going to be tipsy,' she said. 'In fact, I already am! Shall you mind having to help me out of here after the show?'

'No,' he said, 'we'll help one another.'

After that the whole evening began to run together, so that looking back later she was able to recall only vague impressions and isolated incidents. By the time the show came on she was past being shocked or even surprised by the scanty nature of the costumes worn by the well-developed chorus line, enjoying the glitter and dazzle of sequins and ostrich feathers, the lavish scenery and colourful routines. She knew Brendon watched her as much if not more than he watched the girls up there, and found that knowledge strangely exciting.

Occasionally, and then with increasing frequency, she felt her eyes drawn to his, glances that lingered each time and brought tension to her limbs. He was so like Mark, and yet not like him. When had Mark ever looked on her as anything but a child to be protected? Brendon saw her differently, that was apparent. And not as a sister either. It was there in his smile, in the narrowing of his gaze, the lift of an eyebrow. He was attracted to her the same way she was attracted to him.

When he slid an arm about her shoulders she made no protest, leaning her head against him with an audible inhalation of breath. It felt so good to be held close like this, to smell the faint masculine scent of after-shave, to know that hardness of muscle and sinew peculiar only to the male. She wanted him to kiss her; right then she wanted it very badly. Without thinking about it, she turned her face up to his, her whole body awaiting the moment of contact.

Brendon was the first to break it off, lifting his head to look at her with eyes from which all banter had fled. His voice sounded low and rough when he spoke. 'Let's go home.'

She remembered little of the journey, only the warmth and comfort of his support. It was Brendon who found the apartment key in her purse and opened the door; Brendon who took off her coat and turned her into his arms without switching on a light. She kissed him back feverishly, afraid he would stop the way he had last time. Only this wasn't Mark, it was Brendon, she thought in confusion. The same but different. Her head was spinning like a top, the floor itself beginning to move beneath her feet.

Dazedly, she felt herself lifted and carried, laid down again on cushions. The lips at her throat had fire in them, scorching a path down the open V of her neckline until they found the soft swell of her breasts.

'You're lovely,' he murmured against her skin. 'So smooth and warm! Mark should never have left you alone like this.'

'Mark doesn't love me,' she whispered blindly into the darkness. 'Do *you* love me, Brendon?'

He groaned then, a low sound deep down in his throat, pushing himself upwards and away from her. When he spoke it was in tones of self-directed contempt. 'I have to be just about the biggest louse going!'

'If you were you'd have said yes and carried on,' Dana tried to sound realistic about it, but the tremor gave her away. 'It was a silly question anyhow.'

'Not silly,' he said. 'Fortuitous. If you hadn't pulled me up I'd never have been able to look myself in the eye again.' His head turned towards her, the line of his mouth rueful. 'I'm sorry, Dana. That's the closest I ever came to losing my head.'

'It's all right.' Her tone was dull. 'I suppose I asked for it.'

He put out a hand then and touched her cheek. 'That isn't true—not the way you mean it. I should have left you alone in the first place, then it would never have happened.'

'But you had to get back at Mark.'

His laugh came low. 'That's what I told myself yesterday. Only it wasn't true, not wholly. Getting back at Mark was only a minor part of it.' He paused before adding softly, 'You asked me just now if I loved you. Well, the answer is yes. I think it happened the first time I saw you—the day you married my brother. You looked like every man's dream of a dewy-eyed bride.' His tone hardened. 'I could kill him for hurting you!'

'He did what he thought was for the best.' Her own voice was unsteady. 'Brendon, why didn't I meet you first!'

'It's called fate,' he said. 'It's often cruel.' His mouth twisted. 'I wonder what Mark would say if I asked him to have your marriage annulled so that you could marry me? If it comes to that, what would you say?'

'I think I'd say yes,' she said after only a moment. 'You'd be very easy to love.'

He made a move towards her, then checked, shaking

his head wryly. 'That way I'll never get out of here. At least I don't have to imagine you with Mark any longer.'

'But I'll be living with him,' she responded. 'He refuses to consider an annulment inside two years. I don't think he sees me as capable of looking after myself before then.'

'You wouldn't have to if I was doing it for you.' Brendon pointed out. 'There's no way he can hold you against your will.'

'I know.' She was silent for a moment, trying to see things clearly through the fuzziness in her head. 'Why don't we leave it until I'm eighteen? It's only another six weeks.'

His shrug was philosophical. 'I don't suppose we have much choice. What about between times? Do I get to see you at all?'

'It will have to be during the day,' she said, and felt her heart lighten at the thought. 'Unless Mark goes off on any more overnight trips.'

'I'll live in hope.' He studied her a moment longer, then got decisively to his feet. 'I'd better go while my will power is at high water. If I once start kissing you again I'm going to be in trouble. Anyway, you look as if you need to go to bed and sleep it off. That's another apology I owe you—I shouldn't have let you drink so much. Can you manage on your own?'

'Yes, thanks.' Dana had to smile at his assumption of authority. At least with him it wasn't total. 'I think it's going to be quite some time before I drink as much again.'

She went with him to the door, wanting him to stay, knowing he must go. Tomorrow Mark would be back and everything would be as it was before. No, not quite, a small voice whispered comfortingly. She had Brendon now; a man who loved her enough to turn down what could have been a very easy conquest. He didn't think her too young—not for anything.

She clung to him when he kissed her, reluctant even now to be alone. Again it was Brendon who stood back, albeit with reluctance.

'I'll phone you tomorrow,' he said, and went.

They met again the following afternoon. Just for an hour, Brendon had said on the telephone, but it stretched to two. They did nothing special, just walked in the park and sat in a café drinking tea, but for Dana the companionship alone was worth going out on a limb for.

'It's strange,' she said at one point. 'You're still ten years older than I am, yet with you I don't feel it.'

He smiled at that. 'Perhaps because it isn't enough to make me a surrogate father figure.'

It was a moment before she responded, tone uncertain. 'You really think that's all it was?'

'I'm sure of it. Your own father was proving to be rather less than the man you'd thought him, and you needed someone to turn to. Mark was a natural enough choice considering the way he was presented to you. You're not in love with him; you never were in love with him. You just told yourself you were because that made it all easier to accept.' He shook his head at her look of doubt. 'I'm right, Dana, I know I'm right. One day I'll prove it to you.'

'How?' she asked, and he smiled again, reaching for her hand.

'You'll know when the time comes. The day you're eighteen we're going to tell Mark how we feel.'

'Always providing,' she said very softly, 'that you still feel the same way by then.'

'I shall, don't doubt it.' He sounded devoid of the latter emotion himself. 'If there is a question mark at all it has to be you. You're going to have to be sure.'

'I shall be,' she said. 'I'm sure now.' It was almost the truth. 'You're a very special person, Brendon.'

The blue eyes wore a wry expression. 'I was never a particularly patient one, but it appears I'm going to have to be.'

It was gone five when they parted, and another half an hour before Dana arrived home. Dropping her coat on the chaise-longue in her room, she stretched out on the bed to think about the past twenty-four hours and explore her inner self. She was drawn to Brendon without a doubt, both physically and emotionally, but was it enough? If she was to go on seeing him like this she had to know what she wanted—and who.

Not that the latter signified, she acknowledged at that point. What it all boiled down to was that Mark didn't want *her*—not in any sense that mattered—while Brendon did.

She had left her door open when she came into the room, thinking the place empty. When she turned her head a little she saw Mark standing in the doorway looking at her, an odd stillness about him.

'Are you feeling all right?' he asked.

'Yes, fine.' Dana took her time coming upright, aware that she had to find some other plausible reason for lying here dreaming at this time of the evening. 'I'm just a bit tired, that's all. I didn't hear you come in.'

'I've been in over an hour,' he said. 'I got tickets for that musical you wanted to see. I thought we might have an early meal then make tracks for the theatre, but if you're too tired . . .'

'No. No, I'm not.' She swung her feet to the floor and sat up, pushing back her tumbled hair with one hand. 'Mrs Powell will have left everything ready as usual. It won't take long.'

'There's no tearing rush,' he said. 'The show doesn't start till eight.' He paused, making no attempt to come further into the room. 'You were out shopping again?'

'Yes.' The lie was out before she could think, immediately giving rise to another. 'I'm having things delivered. How did your trip go?'

'Better than I anticipated,' he said. 'I'll go and change.'

She drew in a long, slow breath as the door closed behind him, feeling almost as if she had been caught cheating. Yet cheating on what? Theirs was not a real marriage. For all she knew, Mark was seeing Marion again. And even if he wasn't, what difference did it make? They couldn't go on like this for two whole years.

CHAPTER EIGHT

THE show was everything the critics had said of it. Watching the action and listening to the music, Dana was able at times to forget the man who sat at her side and lose herself in the sheer romance of the plot.

'Very much,' she was able to say with truth when Mark asked her if she had enjoyed it on their way home, 'but I know you didn't, so you don't have to pretend.'

'It isn't really my kind of thing,' he admitted mildly enough, 'but I wouldn't go so far as to say I hated it.'

It was a moment before Dana could bring herself to proffer the apology she knew was forthcoming. 'I'm sorry,' she said. 'That must have sounded very ungrateful.'

His shrug bespoke a certain indifference. 'You don't have to feel grateful. It isn't often I have time or opportunity to do something outside my normal interests. It's good for all of us to get out of the rut occasionally.'

They had travelled by taxi because of parking problems. Sitting there in the dimness of the cab, Dana was reminded of the previous night when she had been with Brendon in similar circumstances. The detail was hazy still, but she knew they had been closer than this. Fleetingly she wondered what Mark's reaction might be if she told him about Brendon now. Not that she had any real intention. It was her secret to hug to herself in the lonely hours, her comfort in moments of stress.

'Have you thought about what's going to happen at Christmas?' she heard herself saying without conscious prompting. 'I mean the day itself more than anything, I suppose.'

'We're spending it with my father.' His tone was uncompromising. 'He wants us to stay at the house for a couple of days.'

'And you agreed?'

'I couldn't find any adequate reason not to agree. It's going to be his last Christmas. He knows it, and he's well aware everyone else knows it. Two whole days isn't much of a sacrifice to make.'

'It wouldn't be a sacrifice at all,' she said thickly, 'if it didn't mean lying to him all the time we're there. What do we do about rooms?'

'The same thing we did once before, I imagine.'

Her head came round sharply. 'I don't . . .'

'It won't happen again.' There was tension about his mouth. 'I'll make sure of that. And I'm not asking you, Dana, I'm telling you. We're going to do as he wants.'

She subsided, thankful that the partition was closed between them and the driver. There was little use in arguing when Mark spoke like that; she had learned that much very early on. Yet over two days surely her father-in-law was going to suspect something wrong? Brendon would be there too, in all probability. She wasn't yet sure whether that fact was going to make things better or worse. At least she would know she had his support even if he couldn't come right out and state it.

She told him the news over lunch on the Friday, relieved that he seemed to view the prospect with pleasure rather than trepidation.

'Actually Dad already mentioned it,' he said. 'He's looking forward to having a family Christmas—says it will be almost like old times when Mother was alive. The one missing will be Gary, of course. From what Mark told me, there doesn't seem much chance of his making it home even for a few days. The case still has to come to court.'

'But he'll get off, won't he?' Dana asked. 'Mark said he would.'

'Mark isn't the oracle. Nothing's certain until it happens, especially where it concerns the law. He's hired the best lawyer in the country and that's about all he can do. If Gary lands a sentence we're going to have to face it somehow. The way things are . . .' he stopped, shaking his head . . . 'well, we'll just wait and see.'

Dana knew what he had been going to say. The way things were it was more than possible that Joseph Senior would be beyond hurt by the time Gary went to court. In its own way it would be a blessing.

Brendon was watching her face. 'How is it going?' he asked.

'The same.' She lifted her shoulders in a wry little gesture. 'Mark doesn't change. I don't suppose he ever will.'

His smile warmed her. 'What I can't understand is how any man can be married to a girl like you and leave her strictly alone. I know I couldn't.'

'He doesn't think of me that way,' she said, 'so he doesn't have any problem.'

'I still don't like to think of you living in the same apartment, sharing the same bathroom.'

'I have my own bathroom,' she denied. 'And Mark never comes into my room.' She paused there, struck by a thought. 'What will happen to the house when your father dies?'

'I don't know,' he admitted. 'The lease still has a fair time to run, so I suppose it could be sold—unless Mark plans on moving back there himself. He refused to discuss future plans the other night, except to say there may be some surprises in store. Why? Do you like the idea of living there yourself?'

Dana shook her head emphatically. 'I'd hate it. It's far too big, for one thing.'

'I agree. And the question won't arise if I have my way, because you won't be with Mark.' He lifted her hand to his lips and kissed it, heedless of the indulgent smiles of the people at the next table. The blue eyes were serious. 'I mean it, Dana. I won't let him keep you a moment longer than I have to.'

She made no attempt to withdraw her hand from his grasp, needing the sense of security it gave her. With Brendon she could have a future worth living—a future with a man who loved her and wanted her as Mark never would. She was very close to loving him now; it wouldn't be hard to fall all the way.

Christmas Eve was crisp and clear. Mark went in to the bank in the morning, but was home again by three to pick up Dana and drive over to the house in good time for tea.

Anticipating very little in the way of genuine festive spirit, she was taken totally aback by the sight of the huge and beautifully decorated tree adorning the hall, exclaiming in delighted admiration to Mrs Bartholomew who had opened the door to them.

'Mr Senior's orders,' admitted the latter. 'It's almost like old times having pine needles treading all over the place again.' Her eyes were twinkling. 'Your father's taking a nap,' she added to Mark. 'He said to tell you he'd see you before dinner. Would you like tea in your room, or shall I serve it down here?'

'Down here, I think,' he said. 'Say in fifteen minutes? We'll take ourselves up. Which room have you put us in?'

'Mr Senior said you were to have the master suite,' returned the housekeeper. 'It's high time it was used again. I've had the mattress well aired, and the heating is on, of course. I think you'll find it very comfortable,' the last to Dana.

Dana smiled and made the appropriate responses without looking in Mark's direction. Mattress, the other woman had said. That meant only the one bed. Would they put a pillow down the middle again, she wondered with a hint of cynicism, or would Mark decide this time to occupy a chair? It really made little difference in the long run. She wished Brendon would put in an appearance, yet she dreaded the moment too. She had seen him almost every day this last week, and they had become very close. What they both had to guard against was any hint of that familiarity showing.

The suite was very well appointed, with a dressing room off it in addition to the private bathroom. There was a divan in the former, but it had a day cover on it. Still, it was one answer to the problem, Dana thought. With the heating on she was hardly going to miss a blanket off the bed this time.

Mark made no comment about the sleeping arrangements, unpacking the few items of clothing he had brought with him in the manner of one long accustomed to fending for himself. Dana followed his example, then had a quick wash and brush-up before presenting herself as ready to go down for tea.

There was still no sign of Brendon when they reached the drawing room, although three cups stood ready on the trolley Mrs Bartholomew had drawn up close to the fire. The scent of yew logs permeated the air.

Dana ignored the waiting chairs, curling up on the floor with her hot buttered crumpet to nibble ecstatically while she gazed into the leaping flames.

'One thing Aunt Eleanor always had at Christmas was a yule log fire,' she said. 'We used to bake mince pies on Christmas Eve night so they'd be good and fresh for the church choir when they finished the carol service.'

'Will she be on her own this year?' asked Mark from his seat a few feet away, and she looked round with a smile.

'Hardly. Christmas Day there's always a crowd of people at the house. I've known her invite whole families to spend the day—those whose circumstances make it difficult to celebrate. Last year we had twelve pensioners, all without families of their own.'

'Did you enjoy it?'

Dana pulled a small wry face. 'To be honest, not a lot. Old people can be so demanding. I barely sat down all day.'

'I suppose,' he said mildly, 'there's a certain entitlement attached to age. Your aunt sounds a very well-intentioned woman.'

'Oh, she is! And she does an awful lot of good. I . . .' She broke off as the door opened to admit Brendon, the colour rising involuntarily under her skin. Mark was looking directly at her and must have noted the fact, yet there was nothing in his voice to suggest it.

'I was wondering where you'd got to,' he said, turning his head to follow her gaze.

'Haven't been in long,' answered his brother easily. 'I had some last-minute shopping to do.' His smile was for Dana. 'Hallo, little sister.'

She was in control of herself again now, her laugh light. 'How would you like it if I called you Big Brother?'

'Wrong year,' he said. 'Is Dad not coming for tea?'

'He's resting.' This time there seemed a certain narrowing of the blue eyes as Mark looked across at the younger man. 'He said he'll see us before dinner. Are you going to be here?'

'Of course.' Brendon reached for a crumpet, sliding it on to a plate. 'Pity Gary can't be. It won't be much fun for him where he is.'

'He'll be well looked after.' Mark sounded brusque. 'At least he's still alive.'

'While the girl obviously isn't.' Brendon lifted expressive shoulders. 'Nothing's going to bring her back. Have you heard yet when the case might come up?'

'Mid-January, that's the earliest we could manage. If he's lucky he can be in Maui before the end of the month.'

'You're going to let him manage the estate?'

'He's going to help run it if things work out.'

Brendon eyed him thoughtfully. 'Then you've already found another manager?'

'Let's just say I have one in mind.' The tone was evasive. 'The most difficult part will be getting him here to see Father without giving anything away. He looked a wreck when I saw him in October, but three months should find him reasonably normal again.'

'Maybe one of us should have gone over to visit him.'

Mark shook his head. 'He asked me to keep the family out of it until he's got a hold of himself. He doesn't want to see any of us before then.'

'Fair enough. I didn't much relish the thought of going out there anyway. Particularly not at present.' Once again Brendon's eyes sought Dana's, the smile in them unconcealed. 'I've got to start sorting my own life out pretty soon.'

'Does Gary resemble the two of you?' asked Dana hurriedly, not daring to look at Mark.

It was Brendon who answered. 'No, he's fair and skinny—or at least he was last time I saw him, must be nearly four years ago. He'd just surpassed himself by getting sent down from university after only two months. That was one thing we didn't manage to keep from Dad. Not that it made so much difference. Youthful high spirits, he called it. If it had happened to either of us in our day and time it would have been God help us!'

'You've made your point.' Mark spoke quietly but with purpose. 'Most of us have some kind of blind spot. Gary's given himself a bad time over this girl, and he's still doing it. I think this time the lesson went home.'

'Let's hope.'

Conversation became more general after that, somewhat to Dana's relief. Brendon's attitude towards his brother had undergone a definite and noticeable deterioration, and she knew she was the reason. It was almost as if he intended to give himself away, she thought. But if he did he would be giving her away too, and that she wasn't ready to face. Somehow she had to get him on his own and make him see sense.

Changing for the evening was accomplished without difficulty thanks to the availability of the dressing room. Dana wore blue and left her hair down, tired of trying to look older than she was.

'You look like Alice in Wonderland,' Joseph Senior commented when they reached the library where he was dispensing pre-dinner drinks. His smile held indulgence. 'A very lovely one. Come and give an old man a kiss in return for your sherry.'

Dana obeyed gladly, thinking he actually looked a little better than when she had last seen him. Perhaps after all the medics were wrong. It had happened before. How wonderful if he should confound them all and recover.

Brendon came down shortly after, completing the family group so far as it went. As no comment was made regarding Gary's absence, Dana could only conclude that some reasonably satisfactory explanation had been proffered and accepted. It was to be hoped it would be possible for him to come home soon, but the charge had to be a serious one. Twenty-two and his life already in ruins; it didn't bear thinking about.

She sat on her father-in-law's left at dinner, with Mark opposite and Brendon next to her. The way things were she could almost wish that Brendon had a partner of his own for the evening. At least she wouldn't have felt quite so hemmed in. She had a feeling that Mark was watching the two of them whenever they conversed, yet when she glanced across at him he was usually either eating or talking with his father. Guilty conscience, she decided in the end. Regardless of circumstances, her relationship with Brendon was all wrong, and she knew it. Yet if she gave it up where did that leave her? This last week he had been her lifeline. Without him she had nothing.

They had coffee in the drawing room, with brandy and cigars for the men. Dana declined a liqueur, mindful of the last time she had overstepped her limit. One day she would learn to drink without letting it affect her, she thought wryly, but no doubt it took practice. Everything took practice—including growing up.

'I want to show you something,' her father-in-law said when he had finished his brandy. 'It's in my study. This doesn't include you, Mark.' He got slowly and stiffly to his feet, his only sign of pain in the slight catch of his breath as he moved. 'Come along, my dear.'

Dana accompanied him in some mystification, wondering what on earth he was going to reveal to her. Another collection perhaps? Yet she had understood coins were his only real interest in that direction.

The study lay across the inner hall. He went directly to the wall safe lying behind a Monet landscape on the far wall, extracting a long leather case which he brought to the desk where she stood.

'These belonged to Mark's mother,' he said. 'As you're his wife they should be yours now. They're going to need resetting, but I wanted you to see them first. That dress you're wearing now would make the ideal background for them.'

Dana gasped as he opened the case, unable to believe the sheer beauty of the diamond and sapphire necklet and earrings on the white satin bed. They must be worth a small fortune, she thought dazedly. And he wanted to give them to her! She hardly knew what to say.

'They're lovely,' she got out at last, 'but I really can't accept them. Supposing I lost them!'

'You're hardly going to be wearing them every day,' he returned with dry humour. 'And they're well insured. Jewellery was meant to be worn, Dana. My wife loved this set more than any other. She would have wanted you to have it.'

'I don't deserve it,' she said, and meant every word. Her throat hurt. 'It's too much!'

'I'll be the judge of that.' He took the necklace from the case, setting the stones sparkling as they caught the light from the lamp. 'Let me put it on for you. You can wear it tonight, then let me have it back for resetting.'

'I'd rather it stayed the way it is,' she said, acknowledging the fact that she was going to have to accept the gift. She felt close to tears. 'It's beautiful.'

'We'll talk it over with Mark,' he returned gently. 'Hold your hair up while I fasten the clasp. It always was a rather awkward one.'

Dana put up her free hand to touch the stones as the coldness of them settled about her throat. 'I don't know what to say,' she murmured huskily, 'except thank you.'

'That's enough.' He moved round her to view the piece, leaning his weight against the desk edge behind him as if he needed the support. The gaunt features were softened by the lamplight, giving her a glimpse of the man he might have been had illness not struck. He was smiling as he looked at her. 'I have to admit I still have reservations about this marriage of yours, but at least I can understand why Mark found the temptation so irresistible. You're a very lovely girl, Dana—and not just in looks. There's no guile about you. You are what you seem. I like that.'

Don't, she wanted to say, but the word wouldn't come. Shame choked her. She wasn't what he thought. She wasn't what anyone thought. She was deceiving this man's son with another of his sons. Could anything be worse than that?

It became even more unbearable when he leaned forward to kiss her quickly and fondly on the forehead. For a wild moment she contemplated telling him the whole story, but only for a moment. Confession might relieve her, but it would put an intolerable burden on him. She had to continue the act to the bitter end.

'Come on back and show Mark how you look,' he said.

The brothers were half way down a second brandy apiece, the atmosphere a little charged as if words might have passed between them. Dana kept her eyes fixed on Mark's face as he viewed the necklace about her throat, searching for his reaction without success.

'Time they came out of storage,' was all the comment he made.

'What do you think about the setting?' his father asked. 'Perhaps something a little more modern?'

'It's entirely up to Dana,' he said. 'Personally, I like them the way they are.'

'Then we'll leave them that way,' she stated swiftly. 'I'd prefer it too.'

'It's almost midnight,' Brendon put in. 'If we're going to bring Christmas in properly you two should have a drink.' He stood up to get them, face set in lines Dana recognised as stubborn intent. 'Turn on the radio, someone. That way we'll be sure of the exact moment.'

Dana sat down at Mark's side on the chesterfield as her father-in-law went to obey the injunction. 'I couldn't refuse,' she said thickly. 'He wouldn't let me.'

'You weren't expected to refuse,' he returned without expression. 'I knew what he intended.'

'But you don't approve.' It was a statement, not a question.

'It isn't a matter of approval. It was his choice. I simply think you're too young to wear jewellery of that kind yet.'

'According to you I'm too young for everything,' she retorted, not bothering to keep the bitterness from her voice. 'I'm surprised you haven't put me in a playpen before now!'

'I'll put you somewhere else if you're not very careful,' he threatened. 'Don't press me, Dana. I'm in no mood for it.'

'Where's your festive spirit?' jeered Brendon lightly, coming over with the sherry Dana had asked for in time to catch the last few words. 'Cheer up, man, you're not over the hill yet.'

Perhaps fortunately Mark didn't get the opportunity to answer the crack. Judging from the sudden hard glitter in his eyes retaliation might very well have been harsh. Dana jumped to her feet as the familiar tones of Big Ben began their countdown, her face flushed, voice over-bright. 'Listen! It's almost here!'

Brendon pulled her to him as the last note struck, kissing her full on the mouth. 'Happy Christmas,' he said. He was laughing, the blue eyes full of defiance. 'Now's the time we start getting our New Year resolutions ready.'

Mark had risen too. When he kissed her his lips felt cold and unyielding. Certainly they failed to linger. 'Happy Christmas,' he said.

Joseph Senior came over to complete the greeting, a rueful quality in his smile. 'I'm going to leave you to it,' he announced.

'We're going up too,' said Mark. 'Time enough in the morning for celebrating.' His glance at Dana offered no choice in the matter. 'Ready?'

'I'm staying,' Brendon stated flatly to no one in particular. 'No point in wasting a couple of good logs.'

There was a fire in the bedroom too, despite the central heating radiators. Dana went to sit beside it, waiting for Mark to make the first move towards sleeping arrangements. If he wanted the bed he could have it; she would take the divan herself. Resentment still burned in her.

'Don't sulk with me,' he warned her. 'There's all day tomorrow.'

'Today,' she corrected without looking round. 'And I don't sulk.'

'I'll take your word for it.' He was silent for a moment

and she could feel his eyes on her, then he sighed. 'I'll sleep in the dressing room. Goodnight.'

She didn't stir until the door had closed behind him, conscious of the ache behind her eyes. Things were getting worse, not better. The anger in him had been real. What had Brendon been saying downstairs while she had been with her father-in-law? she wondered. Something had passed between them, it was certain. Yet if he had given her away Mark would surely have taken the matter up with her, wouldn't he? It didn't make sense.

It was around one-thirty before she finally made the decision to try to see Brendon alone. If he had already come upstairs she would just have to go to his room, that was all. She knew which it was. What she was going to say to him when she did see him remained open to doubt. In essence nothing had changed, yet she felt so churned up inside.

The house was silent when she opened her door, but a low light was still on in the hall, suggesting that someone was still up and around. With the cream silk peignoir floating about her ankles, she moved to the head of the staircase and looked over the balustrade. There was a light in the drawing room too; she could see the glow of it under the door. It could only be Brendon in there.

She descended the stairs without a sound in her slippered feet, pausing only a moment when she reached the bottom before going across the expanse of polished tiles to push open the drawing room door. Brendon was sitting with his feet stretched out to the dying flames, a glass in his hand. His smile held relief mingled with something else—gratification, Dana thought. He had waited for her to come to him.

His greeting confirmed the impression. 'I thought you'd never get here. Shut the door, darling, and come over here to the fire. It's the only chance we're going to have to be alone.'

She obeyed neither injunction, standing with one hand resting on the door handle and regret in her heart. She shouldn't have come at all; she knew that now. Her motives in doing so could only be misread.

'I came because I need to know what Mark said to you tonight,' she got out. 'When I was out with your father, I mean.'

'Ah, that.' The smile took on a different slant. 'He told me in no uncertain terms to put a curb on the amount of attention I was paying you. I told you he'd be dog-in-the-manger about you.'

'While I'm still married to him I suppose he has the right,' she said.

'Not if it means coming between us.' He put down the empty glass and got to his feet, coming across to where she stood to take her by the hand and draw her gently into the room, pushing the door to behind her. 'I doubt if I'll ever be able to give you sapphires, but you won't want for love. You're the best thing that ever happened to me, Dana. I won't give you up now.'

She didn't struggle when he kissed her, but neither did she respond. He was taking things too far too fast, she thought numbly. She wasn't ready for this. Yet could she blame him after the way she had acted these past days? She had been willing enough then to deceive Mark.

The sudden reopening of the door almost caught her in the back. Brendon pulled her clear just in time, holding on to her as he looked beyond her to the man framed in the doorway. There was no guilt in his expression, just a certain wry acceptance.

'I think this is what they call the classic situation,' he said.

Dana turned her head slowly to look into Mark's hard features with a sense of fatalism. She was here for reasons other than Brendon was suggesting, but who was going to believe her? Certainly not Mark, judging from his expression.

'Go upstairs,' he said. 'I'll talk to you later.' A muscle jerked at the angle of his jaw when she made no move. 'Dana!'

'You'd better do as he says,' Brendon advised, taking his arm away, and she bit her lip, aware that it would now seem it was him she was obeying rather than his brother. Not that she wanted to obey either.

'Mark . . .' she began, and saw the muscle jerk once more.

'Upstairs,' he repeated. 'I'm not going to say it again.'

She went because there was little else she could do, but she refused to do it in any chastened manner. She had a feeling that Mark was having a hard time keeping his hands off her as she passed him with head held high, but couldn't bring herself to care. Whatever happened, she wouldn't plead for understanding. She doubted anyway if she could put her feelings into words.

It was a good fifteen minutes before he followed her. She was sitting on the bed when he came into the room, her whole body under rigid control. There was no sign of exchanged blows about his features but that didn't necessarily mean a great deal. He was taller than Brendon, and rather more solidly muscled. One well-aimed punch could have laid the other man out for the count.

'Don't look so concerned,' he advised cynically. 'He's still alive and kicking. Whether he stays that way is up to him from now on.' He eyed her for a moment, the blue given way to granite. 'He told me you'd been seeing each other for over a week. Is that true?'

She nodded, unable to trust her voice. Words would be wasted in any case, she imagined.

'And the night I was away,' he went on inexorably. 'You spent that together?'

'No!' This time the word was dragged from her. 'Brendon can't have told you that. He wouldn't!'

There was no flicker of apology in the lean face. 'He didn't. What he did say was that the two of you went out to a nightclub and finished up back at the apartment, where you finally realised just what you meant to each other.' The last on a biting note of satire. 'Suppose you try telling me just what it is he does mean to you.'

Anger erupted in her suddenly, white-hot and flaring. He wasn't even taking her part in this with any real seriousness. He didn't believe her capable of deciding her own emotions. Well, she would show him! She would prove it to him.

'I'm in love with him,' she stated flatly. 'As soon as I can get free of you I'm going to marry him instead. It's what we both want.'

'Just like that?' He sounded coolly derisive. 'And what if I don't choose to allow it?'

'You can't stop it. If you make things difficult I'll simply go and live with him, that's all.'

He drew in a long, slow breath, all semblance of tolerance finally evaporating. 'I think it's about time I slapped some sense into you,' he growled.

Dana curled her lip in deliberate imitation of his own scorn a moment or two ago. 'That underlines the difference between you and Brendon. You see, not only does he treat me as a woman, he knows how to make me react like one. That's something you could never manage! I wonder how Marion would say you compared, if she were honest. I dare you to ask her some time!'

He was very still, the anger in him somehow changed in quality. 'That's enough,' he said without expression.

'No, it isn't enough.' She was past taking warning. 'You're such a big man, Mark, so admired and respected. I wonder how far that respect will go when it becomes known that you couldn't even keep your brand new wife longer than a few weeks?'

She stopped there, held by the glitter in the blue eyes, the purposeful jut of his jaw. She had gone too far, she knew with sudden frightening clarity. Mark had a breaking point after all, and she had found it.

He reached her before she could press herself to her feet, pushing her down on to the bed with hands that hurt and pinning her there while he found her mouth with his. She had felt his weight on her before, but not like this. It crushed her, forcing the breath from her lungs until she had neither strength nor will left to fight.

CHAPTER NINE

She lay like a block of ice when he finally moved away from her, her eyes fixed unseeingly on the ceiling. Her mind felt numbed, the ache in her body a thing detached. It had happened at last, this mystery she had yearned to plumb—the experience denied her on her wedding night. How had she ever imagined it might be enjoyable? she wondered. All she had been aware of was pain and degradation.

It was Mark who broke the silence, his voice low and rough. 'I never meant that to happen—especially not this way. I should have shut you up before you had chance to get to me.'

'I hate you.' She said it without emotion, without feeling of any kind.

'I can hardly expect anything else.' The acknowledgement was rueful. 'There isn't a great deal I can say right now.'

'There's nothing you can say any time that will make any difference!'

'There has to be,' he said. 'It happened and there's no going back, so we have to find a way of living with it.' He got to his feet, reaching for the robe he had dropped by the bed. 'We'll talk about it in the morning.'

Dana stirred then, conscious for the first time of her nudity. He had stripped her of her clothing the same way he had stripped her of her girlhood—ruthlessly and without compunction. 'Go away,' she said, and heard the sudden quiver in her voice. 'Just *go* away!'

'I wouldn't even if I could.' He sat down again on the bed, holding her still as she attempted to roll away from him. 'Dana, listen to me! You've had a bad experience and I'm wholly to blame, but don't for God's sake think it's always like that.'

'It was hateful!' She couldn't control the shudder that ran through her. 'I'll never let another man touch me again!'

'Don't say that.' He took her chin in his hand, forcing her to look at him. 'I'm telling you it doesn't have to be that way.'

'I don't believe you.' Her eyes were wild, filled with detestation. 'You're all animals, the lot of you! It's all Brendon really wanted too.'

'Brendon won't be coming near you,' Mark promised on a harder note. He looked at her for a long, contemplative moment, resolution forming slowly in his eyes. 'The only way to convince you is to show you,' he said. 'I caused the damage, it's up to me to rectify it.'

'Leave me alone!' She hit out at him with all the force she could muster, fiercely elated to feel her knuckles connect with his cheekbone. 'I don't need you to show me anything else ever!'

He ignored both blow and words, bending to put his lips to hers. There was no harshness about them now; he used them lightly, subtly, taking his time, until she began to soften and respond even against her will.

The hand circling her breast was gentleness itself, the slow motion of his thumb across her nipple the only movement. Only when she arched her back involuntarily towards him did he effect a change of tactic, fingers sensitive on her skin as they searched for and found every tiny nerve ending.

She offered no resistance when he lowered his mouth to find the same spots, her hands sliding of their own accord into the thickness of the dark hair, holding him to her. The flicking caress of his tongue was an agony of a special kind. She writhed in his arms, wanting it to stop and to go on at one and the same time. The moan came from deep within her throat, followed by another and yet again another. She couldn't stop it, couldn't even mute it. Every last vestige of control was slipping away from her.

Mark's own breathing had altered pitch, growing faster and heavier by the minute. The gentleness vanished, replaced by a demand that elicited its own response. He said her name, the sound almost a groan on his lips as he kissed her throat, her shoulders and down the soft skin under her arm to her waist. Then he was over her and above her and he was a part of her again, only not like last time, because there was no pain, no sense of intrusion, just soaring, mind-bending pleasure and final shattering release.

It was a long time before either of them moved. Dana wanted to stay this way for ever, secure in Mark's arms, the proud dark head heavy on her shoulder. Whatever he had done to her the first time, this had more than made up for it. As she remembered, her body stirred beneath him, awakened to desires and needs only tentatively sensed before. He could never call her a child again. Not any more. She knew the whole of it now.

'Be still,' he said softly, and lifted his head, the expression in his eyes confusing. 'How do you feel?'

She knew what he was asking—and she knew why. He needed reassurance that he had done the right thing. Her hand came up of its own volition to touch his face.

'You know how I'm feeling,' she whispered. 'You have to know. It was so—different.' She paused there, searching her mind for words that wouldn't come—barely sure of what it was she wanted to say. 'Mark . . .'

'We have to talk,' he said, 'but not like this.' He pushed himself upright, reaching once more for the robe he had discarded, and pulling it around him before standing up. The cream peignoir was on the floor. Picking it up, he held it out to her. 'Put this on, will you. It's less emotive. I can't even think straight while you lie there like that.'

Dana obeyed with hands that trembled a little, wondering just what he was going to say. Nothing could be the same again after this, that was certain, but it was the only thing she was sure of.

Mark didn't look at her again until she had fastened the belt about her waist, taking the chair a few feet away from the bed while he waited. When he did speak it was with a measured quality to his voice, as if he had spent the intervening moments carefully considering his options.

'I think the first thing we have to accept is that an annulment is obviously out of the question now. It's been known to have one granted even after consummation has taken place, but the grounds have to be very special, and I doubt if ours would qualify.' He held up a staying hand as she made to speak. 'No, let me finish. I altered the circumstances, so I have to put matters right again—or as right as they can be. What I have to know is how you feel about me now. You said you hated me. Does that still stand?'

'No.' She had to force herself to the same rationality, aware that everything hinged on her responses to whatever it was he was going to suggest. 'No, I don't hate you, Mark. How can I after——' Her voice died away, warmth touching her cheeks as she met the steady blue gaze.

'What happened between us just now could happen to any two people in similar circumstances,' he said dryly. 'Physically we appear to be tuned. That's good. It makes matters a little easier. You see, I think we're going to have to try to make this marriage of ours work after all.'

Dana was silent for a moment, hardly knowing what to say. It was what she had wanted to hear, but not quite the way she had wanted to hear it. Yet what other way was there? He couldn't tell her he loved her because it wouldn't be true, and truth was important between them right now. She wasn't even all that sure how she felt about him—except for the physical side he had already despatched. But to make a marriage work there had to be other emotions involved, surely. Unless he meant that given time they could grow.

'Do you mean to live together as a real married couple?' she asked at length, still not quite certain of her ground. 'Sharing a room, for instance?'

'And a bed.' His mouth had curved faintly. 'Starting tonight. There seems little point in my going back to the dressing room, considering.' He paused, assessing her reactions. 'If it helps at all, I found making love to you an experience I want to repeat.'

'Tonight?' she asked, and saw his lips twitch.

'That I can't vouch for, but there's every chance. You're a lovely little sensualist, Dana. You learn fast, and you don't seem to have any girlish inhibitions. For me that means we're halfway there already.'

'You mean you wouldn't even be thinking of keeping me if I wasn't uninhibited?'

'Don't put words into my mouth,' he said. 'And leave the cynicism to cynics. Lovemaking plays a large part in any marriage. If that doesn't work there's very little chance that anything else will.' He paused again, waiting for her to answer, his brows lifting interrogatively when she failed to respond. 'So how do you feel about it?'

Doubtful, she wanted to say. There were so many questions she needed to ask. What about Marion, for instance? Had he really been seeing her these last weeks, and if so what did he intend doing about it now? She couldn't bring herself to form the words.

'What do I tell Brendon?' she said instead.

His lips tightened suddenly and ominously. 'You don't tell Brendon anything. If I catch him so much as looking at you from now on I'll take him apart!'

'It wasn't all his fault,' she protested. 'I did my share of encouraging, I suppose.'

'I've made some allowance for that already, and you'll hardly be doing it again.' The statement was flat and unemotional, and all the more meaningful for it. 'Do you want to try?'

'Yes,' she said, casting doubt aside. She was suddenly shy of meeting his eyes. 'Yes, I want to try, Mark.'

'That's good.' He came to his feet again, his smile faint. 'Considering the time, we'd better get some sleep, or we're neither of us going to be fit for anything in the morning. Would you prefer I wore pyjamas in bed? I don't normally bother, but I do have some with me.'

'I don't mind.' Her voice sounded husky. 'I don't suppose it matters very much now.'

'I don't suppose it does,' he agreed. 'Leave your nightdress off too. I want to hold you the way nature intended.'

It felt good to lie in his arms like that, she had to admit. His skin was warm to her touch, the muscle hard-ridged across back and shoulders, the hair on his chest less wiry than it looked, creating a pleasant tickle. This man was her husband in every sense of the word now, and while he might not love her yet as she would want him to do they had at least made a start in the right direction. Her own emotions were too complex to be easily defined. Like Mark, she would wait and see what developed between them. At least now their relationship had some meaning.

'Go to sleep,' he murmured softly, sensing something of her circling thoughts. 'Tomorrow's a whole new day.'

Dana woke to the light of it around eight, unable to believe in that first moment of consciousness that last night had not been a dream. Mark had gone from the bed, but she could hear the sound of a razor at use in the bathroom. What had been his thoughts on waking this morning? she wondered. He was stuck with her now. Did he regret it? She might not know even when she saw him. He was too adept at concealing his inner feelings.

Thinking about last night brought a curling sensation deep down in the pit of her stomach. A sensualist, he had called her, and she felt it. She wanted him again; right now, this very minute. If he would come and take her in his arms again she would know at least that much relief from doubt.

She was still lying there when he did come out of the bathroom, the sheets pulled up high under her armpits so that only her shoulders showed above them. Clad once more in the silk robe, he came over to the bed, looking down on her with a smile on his lips.

'Good morning,' he said. 'Would you like some coffee? There's a percolator in the dressing room. It should be just about ready by now.'

Dana shook her head, shyness sweeping over her. Last night they had slept naked in each other's arms; looking at him now it scarcely seemed possible. Could this tall, dark, controlled man really have done what he had done to her, said what he had said to her? In the morning light she could see the faintest flecks of grey at his temples. Somehow that served to make him seem even more remote from last night's lover.

'I have to get up,' she said. 'We're going to be late for breakfast.'

'Bartie will be putting it on the hot tray so we can all help ourselves.' He sat down on the bed edge the way he had in the night, leaning to kiss her with a purposefulness that set bells jangling in her heart again. 'We have all the time in the world,' he murmured against her cheek. 'All it takes is the inclination.'

Making love in the morning was just as pleasurable as by night, Dana found over the following emotive moments. She knew no restraint, responding blindly to his lips, to his hands, to instinct itself. In this way, if not in any other, she had power over him. Regardless of everything, she had made him want her.

It was well gone nine by the time they got downstairs. Joseph Senior was already seated at the breakfast table along with his younger son, neither long arrived themselves, judging from their plates. On impulse, Dana went over and pressed a swift kiss to her father-in-law's thin cheek. 'Good morning,' she said. 'I hope you slept well.'

'As a matter of fact, I did,' he replied. 'The best night I've had in a long time.' He was smiling as he looked up at her, taking in the sparkle in her eyes, the warm clarity of her skin. 'You're a tonic in yourself!'

'It's Christmas,' she laughed. 'I'm high on festive spirit!' The laughter faded as she turned her head to meet Brendon's gaze. He knew, she realised. How, she wasn't sure, but there was no mistaking the expression on his face. 'Good morning to you too,' she said, bluffing it out, and went to join Mark at the hot tray on the sideboard.

The exchange of presents took place in front of the drawing room fire after they finished breakfast. Watching Mark open hers, Dana wished with all her heart that she had taken a little more time and trouble over it, but he seemed pleased enough with the silver-backed hairbrushes.

'Clever of you to notice my old ones were ready for replacement,' he commented, putting them back into the hide case again.

Sheer luck was nearer the mark, but she had no intention of saying so. Next Christmas she would get him something special. The thought that there was going to be another Christmas was enough for the moment.

Her father-in-law's present of a monogrammed silk dressing gown had been Mark's suggestion to come from them both. He exclaimed over it with pleasure that paid no heed to the lack of opportunity he might have to get real use from it, donning it over his shirt sleeves in order to break it in, as he put it, and sitting in it for the rest of the morning.

The cashmere sweater for Brendon had also been Mark's idea. Aware that parcels might well be opened en masse, she had left it at that, afraid of giving too much away if she chose an extra gift. He, apparently, had known no such fear. For Mark there was a leather-bound edition of Chaucer's *Canterbury Tales*, but for Dana herself he had bought an antique silver bracelet which must have cost an appreciable amount of money. More the kind of gift a man might give a wife or fiancée, she thought in dismay when she opened it. She hardly knew what to say.

'It just seemed suitable at the time,' was all the comment Brendon made when she attempted to thank him. He had been very quiet all morning, the blue eyes lacking in their normal liveliness. Meeting hers now they took on a darker hue, asking her a question to which she could not supply an answer. The time for explanations would have to come, that was certain, but it would have to be when Mark was unlikely to be around.

Mark's present she had left until last. Viewing the double string of perfectly matched seed pearls, she felt a lump come into her throat. Last night his father had given her sapphires, but these meant so much more. She insisted on his fastening them about the neck of her cream wool dress there and then.

'Pearls for tears,' Brendon remarked on a note of cynicism. 'I'm going to have a drink. Anyone want to join me?'

The rest of the day passed pleasantly through its stages. Somewhat to Dana's relief there was little opportunity to face Brendon alone. They were changing for dinner when Mark made his first reference to the silver bracelet.

'Give it to me and I'll return it to him,' he said with a hint of brusqueness. 'It's a good piece. Wherever he bought it from they should take it back.'

'Aspreys,' Dana supplied. 'The box says Aspreys.' She hesitated a moment, trying to read his expression. 'Mark, I didn't know he planned on buying me a present at all, much less such an expensive one. You must have realised that when I opened it.'

'I realised you must have given him good enough cause to believe you'd find it acceptable,' he responded. 'Just how much did you tell him about us?'

Dana bit her lip. She could lie about it, of course, but lies had a habit of catching up with one. 'Everything,' she admitted. 'I had to have someone to talk to.'

'My brother was hardly an ideal confidant.'

'He seemed it at the time. He never once tried to run you down to me.'

'Just planned on taking you right out from under my nose.' His tone was dry. 'You certainly have a way with you, Dana. You had him hog-tied in little more than a week. Even last night he was still convinced he could get you to come to him.'

The sudden stab of doubt was like a knife wound in her heart. Was that why he had claimed her for himself? Dog-in-the-manger, Brendon had called him. If that was true he had made love to her only to spite his brother.

No, she wouldn't accept that, she told herself fiercely. The first time she had driven him to it herself, and the rest had stemmed directly from that moment. If Brendon had played a part at all, it was simply that of a catalyst bringing them together at last.

'I must try and explain to him,' she said unhappily. 'I never meant to hurt him in any way.'

Mark's lips thinned. 'You won't explain anything to him. From now on you don't even see him unless I'm there. Do you understand?'

She gazed at him with eyes gone still and dark, noting the implacability of his expression. It would be easy to say yes and accept his ruling, but what kind of precedent

would that set for their future relationship? She was his
wife but not his property.

'I can't promise that,' she said at length. 'I owe him
some explanation, and it would obviously be better
without you there.'

'I said no!' Mark hadn't raised his voice, but there
was no doubting his seriousness. 'He isn't going to get
the chance to put his hands on you again.'

Dana sighed and gave in, recognising the need for
diplomacy at a moment like this. She didn't want to
anger him again. Not so soon. 'I suppose you're right.'

'Right or wrong isn't the issue. I don't want you to
see him. That should be enough.'

'It is.' She went to him then, sliding her arms about
his waist and leaning her cheek against his chest. 'Mark,
don't let's quarrel.'

'Quarrels are for children,' he said. 'Adults have
rows.' His hand lifted to stroke her hair, the other
coming round her to hold her. There was a certain wry
acknowledgement in his voice. 'Bear with me. I'm not
accustomed to sharing decisions.'

Especially not with a child, she thought. He still
saw her that way, despite all that had happened between them. It was up to her to change her image. The
eyes she turned up to his were luminous, her mouth soft
and full. She saw his expression undergo a visible
change, felt the alteration in pace of his heartbeats.
Stretching, she put her arms up about his neck and her
mouth to his, kissing the way he had taught her with
feather-light movement of lips against lips, teasing
him with seeming withdrawal only to press herself to
him in instant response the moment he attempted to
follow her.

'I said you learned fast,' he murmured thickly, 'but I
didn't realise just *how* fast. You're going to wear me
out, do you know that?' He laughed suddenly, sliding
an arm beneath her knees to lift her bodily from the

ground. 'But it's going to be a lovely way to go!'

They went home on Boxing Day after lunch. To Dana even the apartment seemed different somehow. Moving her things into the master bedroom, she thought happily of the night to come when she would share Mark's own bed for the very first time. In his arms she could forget everything but the moment itself—and make him forget too, she was sure. What could Marion have possibly given him that she could not? They had it all.

There had been no opportunity to speak to Brendon at any time because Mark had made certain none arose. Hearing his voice on the phone that first morning Mark went back to the bank came as no real surprise.

'I have to see you,' he said. 'You can't deny me that much, Dana. I have a right to hear it from your own mouth.'

She had to agree, even though it meant defying Mark. There were times in life when one was unable to avoid the small white lie, and this was one of them. With any luck she need never actually have to tell it, anyway.

They met in the restaurant where they had lunched that very first day. Brendon looked drawn, she thought, his normal insouciance totally missing.

'I've been having some late nights,' he admitted when she commented on the fact. His smile lacked humour. 'Trying to forget a certain little girl who's given me a bad time.'

'I'm sorry,' she said with sincerity. 'I really *am* sorry, Brendon. I gave you entirely the wrong impression.'

'Not at the time, you didn't,' he insisted. 'It was the way you felt.' He studied her, taking in the youthful glow of her hair and skin, the air of confidence she had lately acquired. 'If I didn't want to believe it before I have to believe it now,' he added with wryly bitter inflection. 'You've lost that innocent look. Not that I can blame Mark too much for that. Even he must have his limits.'

'I didn't come here to talk about Mark and me,' she said. 'I came to explain. I was very unhappy and you helped take me out of it, but that was really all it ever was.'

'What about the times I kissed you?' he demanded. 'The way you responded to me? That wasn't all make-believe. You wanted me to want you.'

'I know. It was a kind of—reassurance, I suppose.' She felt wretched, but it had to be gone through. 'Being rejected on one's wedding night isn't an easy thing to get over. I had to know I could make other men want me even if Mark didn't.'

'Except that he apparently did and was simply playing the good guy.' The pause held deliberation. 'Did it occur to you to wonder just what did change his mind?'

Dana met his eyes steadily. 'I know what changed his mind, and it isn't something I'm prepared to discuss.'

'Because you don't want to face it,' he said. 'I told you what would happen when Mark found out about us. No way was I going to steal his property.'

'I'm *not* his property!' Her tone had sharpened. 'He's my husband, not my keeper!'

'Try going against him and see how he reacts.'

'As a matter of fact, I already have.' She was too intent on proving him wrong to pay heed to what she was giving away. 'He told me I wasn't to see you again—but here I am.'

'So you are.' Brendon's regard narrowed for a moment, then cleared again. 'You realise you'll be in trouble if he ever finds out? He'll probably put you across his knee!'

'He probably will,' she agreed lightly, refusing to allow him to annoy her. 'I'll just have to grin and bear it, won't I?'

His mood altered again, his hand reaching out across the table to take hold of hers. 'Dana, I'm not going to give you up. I love you, I want you, and I'm going to make every effort to prove to you that I'd be better for you than Mark.'

She gazed at him helplessly, lost for the words to convince him. 'If you're going to talk like that I think I'd better go,' she said at last.

'All right.' He was instantly penitent. 'I got carried away for a moment, that's all. If you'll stay I promise I shan't mention the subject again.'

Already half risen from her seat, Dana subsided again with some slight reluctance. She still felt enough for Brendon to make it difficult to cast him totally aside, she had to admit. He had been there when she had needed someone, if only for a short time, and that had to count for a lot. By his own admittance he loved her, therefore it stood to reason that he was going to do her no harm. At least they could part friends.

'In that case,' she said, 'I'll stay.'

He seemed more like the Brendon she had first known when he put her into a taxi later. Enough so for her to make no particular objection when he bent forward to kiss her lightly on the lips before he closed the door. He had not suggested meeting her again, which suggested acceptance of the situation the way it was. It was sad in so many ways that it had ever happened. She was going to miss him.

Gary came home in mid-January, a thin and pale young man with a haunted look about his eyes. Meeting him for the first time, Dana was struck by his air of detachment. It was as though he occupied a little world all of his own and had no desire to rejoin theirs.

'He'll come round given time,' Mark advised when she mentioned the matter to him. 'The shock went deep.'

'But surely your father must guess something is wrong,' she insisted. 'He can't always have looked like that.'

'He knows Gary's been ill, that's all—a viral infection

he picked up before Christmas. It was the only way of explaining his failure to be here for the holiday. What Gary needs now is rest and relaxation in a warm climate, only he's refusing to go under the circumstances.'

Dana didn't need ask what those circumstances were. If Gary went to Hawaii now he would most likely never see his father again.

'Was it very difficult?' she asked tentatively, looking at Mark through the dressing table mirror as she brushed her hair prior to retiring for the night. He was already in bed and lying propped on an elbow while he glanced through a sheaf of paperwork brought home with him earlier. 'To get him released, I mean.'

'Enough,' he admitted without looking up. 'And that's a side of the affair we're going to forget from now on.'

'I'm sorry.' Her tone was subdued. 'I didn't mean to pry.'

He sighed then, and lifted his head, expression softened. 'And I didn't mean to sound quite so brusque about it.' One arm stretched to deposit the papers on a side table. 'Come on to bed.'

Later, lying in the darkness with the warmth of his arm about her, she murmured softly, '*Is* it working, Mark?'

It was a moment before he answered her, his tone quiet and unrevealing. 'It takes time. Most worthwhile things do. It might have been easier if we'd been able to follow the original plan and go out to Maui this month, but the way things are . . .'

'I know.' Her heart felt heavy. 'I thought he looked so much better on Christmas Day, but it didn't last. It's feeling so helpless that's the worst part.'

'For us all,' he agreed, and kissed her. 'Stop thinking about it and go to sleep.'

More easily said than done, she thought. Mark wasn't happy—not deep down happy where it mattered. True, one could hardly expect it with his father in the state he was, but it went beyond that. He was missing Marion, she believed; missing the companionship of a mature woman. No matter how satisfactory he found her in bed, she could never provide the same mental stimulation. Some day he was going to get bored with her, and then what? She didn't want to think about that.

CHAPTER TEN

JOSEPH Senior died in his sleep on the third of February, two days after Dana's eighteenth birthday. Exactly one week after the funeral, Mark Senior electrified the City by declining the chairmanship to which he had been elected by a majority of seven votes to four. He was leaving the bank altogether, he stated in the one media interview he granted, to follow a long-standing ambition in taking on the management and running of the family estate in Hawaii. His wife and youngest brother would be going with him.

'I had to do it this way,' he said to Dana when the first furore was over. 'It would have hurt Dad too much if he'd realised that none of his sons fully shared his professional zeal.'

'But you were so good at your job,' she protested. 'Everyone says so! You were the one the Board chose for their chairman.'

'I have a maxim,' he said, smiling a little. 'If a thing is worth doing at all, it should be done to the best of one's ability. I haven't exactly hated my life-style up to now, it just hasn't fulfilled me the way I felt it should.'

That rather accurately summed up his marriage too, she thought with dull acceptance. Going out to Maui would make little difference. She would still be the same person.

'How do you feel about living out there permanently?' he asked now, watching her face.

'Do I have a choice?' she countered, and was at once regretful. 'I really don't mind,' she added swiftly. 'It sounds a lovely part of the world.'

'Painted for you by Brendon it couldn't be anything

143

else.' There was irony in his smile. 'He always had a
way with words.' He turned away from her then to reach
for the whisky glass he had placed on the table at his
side. 'You do realise he won't be coming with us?'

'Of course.' She kept her tone expressionless. 'Just
you and me and Gary. Brendon has his own life to lead.'

The three of them left England together on the twen-
tieth, made an overnight stop in Los Angeles and flew
on to Honolulu the following morning. Expecting to
take a local flight directly from there to Maui, Dana
was surprised but gratified to find that Mark had
reserved rooms out at Waikiki beach for a couple of
nights in order, as he said, to give them all an opportunity to adjust to the time difference before journey's end.

Looking out from the thirtieth floor of their hotel on
the superb view over Diamond Head, she could scarcely
believe that she was actually here in the Hawaiian
Islands and not living a dream. The beach down there
looked like something on a picture postcard, the sand
so white, the sea so blue, the palms waving lazily in the
offshore breeze. Commercialised, perhaps, but surprisingly unspoiled with it.

'Tomorrow we'll take a run out to the Cultural
Centre,' Mark said, coming up behind her. 'It's important to know something about the Polynesian way of
life both past and present if you're going to live here any
length of time. You'll find the language fun to learn
too. Although there's no real necessity as everyone
speaks English.'

'I'm looking forward to learning about the islands,'
she said. 'Including the language.' She leaned her
head back against his chest, aware of a new-found
confidence now that they were so far from other com-
parisons. 'I'm going to love it here, Mark. I'm sure of
it.'

His hands came about her waist, their touch familiar.

'Maui isn't like this. It's quieter, less developed. What night life there is centres around the resort hotels, and there aren't too many of those.'

'It sounds like paradise.' Her tone was dreamy, her senses alive to the hard strength of him at her back. 'Is it too early to go to bed?'

He laughed softly, putting his lips to the lobe of her ear. 'You're insatiable, do you know that?'

'I know.' She said it without shame. 'And who made me that way?'

'Nature laid the groundwork, thank God. One thing I couldn't take would be a wife who suffered from headaches.'

'I never have headaches,' she said, quite seriously, and heard his sudden chuckle.

'You know, I can't always decide whether you're playing me up or not. The kind of headaches I'm talking about are a euphemism for plain reluctance to comply with advances made.'

'Really?' She twisted her head to look at him, not all that sure that he wasn't joking. 'Why not just say it, then?'

'Because not all female minds work on the same principle as yours, my sweet.' He brought her round the whole way to face him, drawing her closer to him and nuzzling his face into her hair. 'What were you saying about bed?'

Gary had improved a little over the past couple of weeks, but he still had to be persuaded to leave his room and come out with them to dinner.

'You two should be alone,' he kept saying. 'You don't need a third party tagging along.'

'We can be alone any other time,' Dana told him with the unequivocality she had found worked the best. 'Right now we both want you with us, so why don't you stop arguing and just come along?'

'Better do as she says,' Mark advised, amusement in

his voice. 'She doesn't believe in taking no for an answer.'

The smile was fleeting, but it was at least a smile. 'In that case I suppose I better had.'

Getting Gary to talk in anything more than monosyllables was something of a task still, but by sheer perseverance Dana was beginning to win through. She felt sympathy for him regardless of what he had done, because he wasn't the tearaway she had anticipated. Not now, at any rate. He was putting himself through some kind of private hell and wasn't yet ready to share it. When he could that would be the day he started to recover.

They were on the beach when it finally happened. Mark had gone surfing, leaving the two of them drinking Piña Coladas and soaking up the sun between the occasional and short-lived showers common to winter in this part of the world.

How it started, Dana couldn't afterwards clearly remember. One minute she was chatting on about sundry items, the next Gary was spilling out the whole sad story. He had loved the girl whose death he had caused, she gathered. They had been lovers for several months before the terrible event. The crowd they had both spent the summer moving around Europe with had included one or two who embraced every experience, beneficial or otherwise, just because it was there to be experienced. They had started him on the drugs which had wrecked his life, and very nearly his health.

'I'm not blaming anyone but myself,' he said towards the end. 'I had a choice. Nobody forced me. The worst part of all was that June wasn't on them—she never had been. Yet she died and I lived. Does that seem fair to you?'

'I don't think life is ever particularly fair,' Dana said carefully. 'And trying to work out why is a thankless

task anyway. If June loved you as much as you loved
her, she wouldn't want you to spend the rest of your life
doing penance. You've punished yourself enough, Gary.
It's time you put it behind you.'

'You know,' he said gruffly, not looking at her,
'Mark's a lucky guy.' His grin was as sudden as it was
unexpected. 'Mind you, what you see in an old man like
him I can't imagine!'

Mark was coming back up the beach towards them
even as he spoke. Viewing the lean and muscular figure,
Dana felt a lump come into her throat. 'I love him,' she
said, and this time knew it was the truth.

Maui was just as it had been described to her, both
by Brendon and by Mark. They came in through the
mountains, at times flying so close to the verdant green
heights it seemed almost possible to reach out and touch
them. The plantation lay inland towards the north of
the island. Driving through, it appeared to Dana to
cover a vast acreage. Pineapples did not, as she had
vaguely imagined, grow on trees, but on plants set low
to the ground in row after cultivated row. Men and
machinery were at work in the fields.

The house was a single-storeyed delight, its rooms
large and airy, its furnishings fitted to the climate. There
was a swimming pool too, she was pleased to see, plus a
surrounding patio ideal for outdoor eating. She liked
every aspect of the place.

'It's like living in heaven!' she exclaimed over a delici-
ous supper cooked and served by the resident staff. 'I
feel like a queen!'

'You eat more like a horse,' commented Gary with
a brotherly candour newly acquired. 'The amount you
can put away, you should be as fat as Lani here,'
grinning at the enormous Hawaiian woman just
bringing out the concoction of exotic fruits which was
their desert. 'A girl has to be big to be beautiful, right,
Lani?'

'Only for our own men,' came the comfortable reply. 'And you stop that teasing, Mr Gary, or I'll box your ears the way I used to when you were a boy!'

'Still the same old Lani!' The chuckle was good to hear. 'Did she treat you the same when you came here as a kid, Mark?'

His brother laughed and shook his head. 'She was younger and thinner then; didn't have the same presence. Aren't you about due for retirement, Lani? Your eldest son must be getting on for my age.'

'What would I do with retirement?' she asked, serving him from the dish.

'More to the point,' he smiled, 'what would *we* do without you? Forget I spoke.'

'It's forgotten,' she said, her serenity quite undisturbed.

That first evening set the pattern for others to come, long and leisurely and without constraint. It was the days which began to be irksome. Alone for much of them while the two men got to grips with the business of running the plantation, Dana swam and sunbathed and wished she could join them. Even paradise began to pall a little when there was no one to share it with.

'I have to find something to do,' she told Lani towards the end of that first week. 'I've read until I'm tired of reading, and I can't just laze around the whole time. Surely there's something I can do?'

The big woman shook her head, dark eyes indulgent. 'When the *keikei* comes there will be enough to do.'

The word needed no explanation. Dana stared at her, wondering how Lani could possibly have known what she herself was only just beginning to suspect.

'I see it written in your face,' came the unasked-for reply. 'There's no doubt about it. It will be a son. Don't ask me how I know that because I couldn't tell you, but I'm never wrong.'

A baby boy. Thinking about it brought a surge of emotion so strong Dana could scarcely contain it. Mark's son, small and helpless; dependent entirely on her. She wanted it to be true. In that moment she wanted desperately for it to be true.

Concern over Mark's possible reaction came later when she had time to rationalise her emotions. They had never talked about children, but he must have realised the likelihood of her becoming pregnant. Of course he would be pleased. Delighted, in fact. What man wouldn't be? All the same, she decided, it might be better to wait until it was medically confirmed before giving him the news, even though that would mean telling Lani not to mention the subject in front of him. Better a delay than a disappointment.

She was making excuses and she knew it, yet she couldn't have explained her reasons. It was as if a sense of foreboding suddenly hung over her—a premonition of bad times to come. She could only hope her fears were unfounded.

Only when Sunday came round did the brothers allow themselves a break from routine, and that reluctantly, on Mark's part at least.

'It can't have been much fun for you,' he apologised to Dana over breakfast, 'but unfortunately there hasn't been any choice. That man Brendon put in charge just left the whole affair to run itself from the state of things. If I knew where he'd gone from here I'd take his salary out of his worthless hide!'

'Perhaps as well you don't, then,' put in Gary dryly. 'The last thing we need is a G.B.H. in the family. Brendon's the one at fault for not making sure of the guy before he stuck him with the job, and as he's not here to answer for his sins I'd say we should forget it.'

Mark's grin was sudden, his anger vanishing. 'I daresay you're right. What's done is done. Let it lie. How about heading for the beach this morning? We could take a picnic lunch.'

Gary's gaze flickered briefly to Dana and back again. 'Not for me, thanks, but you two go ahead.'

They drove to Hana on the east coast through scenery of such splendour and variety it held Dana spellbound. On the one hand lay black sand beaches and isolated fishing villages, while to the other were the slopes of the volcano with old lava flows still in occasional evidence amidst the lush groves of mango and monkey pod trees. There were waterfalls everywhere, it seemed, ranging from tinkling trickles to sparkling cascades.

'I'll take you up to Haleakala one day soon,' Mark promised. 'Preferably in time to see dawn break over the crater. There's no sight quite like it.'

'What does Haleakala mean?' Dana asked.

'The House of the Sun,' he said. 'There's a legend that says the days were once only three or four hours in length because the sun was so fond of sleeping it used to race across the sky in order to get back to bed as soon as possible, until Maui himself caught it by its sixteen legs one morning as it lifted itself over the crater rim and made it promise to walk slowly across the sky in future before he would let it go.'

'Maui was a god?'

'Apparently only a demigod—a mortal, in fact. He's said to have been killed trying to steal the secret of eternal life from the Guardian of the Night so that he could give it to mankind.' Mark smiled and shook his head. 'The islands are a wealth of tales like that. I'd say they rival the Greeks any day when it comes to mythology.'

The cove they eventually chose was quiet and secluded. Relatively few cars found their way round this part of the coast, by all accounts. Mark took binoculars from the car and showed her the humpback whales which had their breeding grounds in the Alenuihaha channel. Beyond that was the island of Hawaii itself, and beyond that again nothing but ocean for two and a half thousand miles.

They swam together before starting on the lunch Lani had packed for them. Lying back on the sand under the shade of a coconut palm after they had finished eating, Dana thought about March gales and driving rain, and felt no great desire to return to England. She had spoken with her father before leaving, but the relationship had deteriorated too far for any real attempt at reconciliation. He had, however, set her mind at rest to a certain extent by assuring her that the loan would this time be redeemed in full. She hoped she could believe him.

Mark was sitting upright with his arms resting on bent knees as he looked out to sea. Seen in semi-profile, his features stood out strongly against the light: the hard-boned ridge of his nose, the firm lines of mouth and jaw. So male, she thought, watching him, and he's mine. But not wholly, came the immediate reminder. You only know his body, not his heart.

Now would have been the perfect time to tell him about the baby had she only been able to convince herself to do it. There was no doubt left in her mind that it was true, yet still she held back. When the time came that she had to tell him he was going to want to know why she had waited so long, and she wasn't going to be able to answer because she didn't really know the answer. It was as if some deep-down instinct held her chained.

The turn of his head caught her unawares, giving her no time at all to mask her emotions. From the faint narrowing of his eyes it was obvious that she had given something of her inner conflict away.

His question confirmed it. 'What were you thinking about just now. You looked almost desperate!'

'I am,' she said swiftly. 'Desperate for you to kiss me.'

He smiled then and leaned towards her. 'That's easily remedied.

'Not that I believe it,' he added softly some moments later, his lips at her throat. 'If you've got something worrying you I should know about it.'

'It's nothing.' The moment the lie was out Dana wanted to retract, but it was already too late. All she could do was repeat it. 'It's nothing.'

'All right.' He sounded just a little short. 'If you don't want to tell me you don't want to tell me. Whatever it is it can't be such a problem.'

'It isn't,' she assured him. 'Just something I have to work out for myself.' She put her hands both sides of the lean face, looking fiercely into his eyes. 'I want you, Mark!'

'Hussy,' he said, but the glow was already there. 'One of these days I'm going to teach you to wait till you're asked!'

They drove back to the house in the late afternoon, not hurrying because there was nothing to hurry for. Curled contentedly in her seat, Dana thought that she would remember this day for a long time to come: the warmth, the dappled shade of the waving palm fronds, the shifting sand settling beneath her. The doubts had cleared in her mind, leaving her aware of what she must do. Tonight she would tell Mark the truth and trust she could make him understand her reticence—make herself understand it too, if it came to that. He was her husband and her lover; of course he would want the baby.

The sun was already setting by the time they reached the plantation, the colours beginning to spread across the western sky in ever-changing patterns as the clouds moved. A strange car stood on the gravel driveway before the house. Mark groaned when he saw it.

'Who the devil can this be! I was looking forward to a long, leisurely soak before supper.'

Gary was out on the patio with the visitors—a woman

and a man, Dana noted from the doorway. She felt the dryness come into her throat as they both turned in unison, sensed the sudden tension in the man at her side and knew with numbing certainty that this was her premonition come to pass.

Marion was the first to break the stillness, her eyes only for Mark. 'Hallo,' she said softly. 'We were beginning to think you'd got yourselves lost.'

'You should have let us know you were coming,' he returned with iron control, looking at his brother. 'I was under the impression you'd washed your hands of this place.'

'I got homesick,' Brendon replied. 'Three years is a long time to just rub off the slate. I thought seeing it again might help me get things into proper perspective.' His gaze moved to Dana, softening in the process. 'Hi!'

She said tonelessly, 'I'd better tell Lani to have rooms made up.'

'It's already done,' Gary put in. He had retreated within himself again, as if reluctant to have anything to do with this new development beyond what was absolutely necessary. Having said that he shut up like a clam.

Marion still hadn't so much as glanced in Dana's direction. Her attention was wholly for Mark. 'I hope you don't mind me coming along with Brendon,' she said. 'He needed company, and I was ready for a break. Anyway, we'd both had enough of being enemies.'

'Why should I mind?' The question had an edge. 'He's perfectly entitled to ask who he wants to visit with him. Let me top you up that glass. I could do with a drink myself. Dana?'

'I have to change,' she said through stiff lips. 'Excuse me, will you.'

She shut the door when she reached the bedroom, leaning against it to take a grip on herself. It was no use closing her eyes to the truth. She had felt the change in Mark the moment he had seen the woman he had once planned to marry. Marion had known it too; it had been right there in her. It might be Brendon she had come with, but it was Mark she wanted.

She only just made it to the bathroom before she was violently sick.

Mark came in some minutes later to find her lying listlessly on the bed. Minutes after that she was undressed and under the covers, with Lani fussing round her like a mother hen. Mark had stood by throughout the operation without offering to help—not that the Hawaiian woman had needed it. Only now did he come over to the bed to put a hand to her hot and sticky forehead.

'You're running a fever,' he said. 'Perhaps we should send for the doctor.'

Dana shook her head, wishing she hadn't as pain lanced through it. 'I'm feeling much better. Probably I had a touch too much sun this afternoon.'

'Perhaps.' The blue eyes were impossible to read. 'All right, so we'll see how you are in the morning.' His lips looked thin. 'Try to get some sleep.'

She did eventually, through sheer exhaustion, wakening only when Mark came to bed. Even then she couldn't bring herself to acknowledge his presence, watching him through slitted eyelids until he turned out the light and slid between the sheets. He made no attempt to touch her, lying on his side with his back turned towards her. He was thinking about Marion, she told herself, staring dry-eyed into the darkness; beautiful, clever Marion whom he should have married instead of her. The comparison had already begun.

It was late when she awoke again, the sun already high above the trees. Nausea swept through her the moment she lifted her head from the pillows, sending her stumbling hastily to the bathroom once more. If there had been any doubt at all as to her condition there was little enough now, she acknowledged weakly when the spasm was over and she could start to think about getting dressed. She had to tell Mark. It was his right to know. She *had* to tell him!

Far from telling him anything she couldn't even look at him when he came into the room while she was dressing. He didn't come near her, standing just within the closed doorway with his hands in the pockets of his slacks.

'How do you feel?' he asked.

'I'm fine,' she said. 'I thought you had to see someone at the canning factory today?'

'I do. I'm leaving right now.' The pause was brief. 'Gary went an hour ago.'

'That's all right.' She kept her tone level by sheer effort of will. 'I'll take care of our guests. Though I shouldn't really call Brendon that, should I? I suppose he has as much right to be here as you and Gary.'

'Just as much,' came the taut agreement. 'They're both in the pool at present. I'll be back around four.'

It was all gone, Dana thought achingly when the door had closed behind him. The Mark of yesterday and the Mark of today were two different people. How did she tell a stranger she was to have his child?

Both Brendon and Marion were in the water splashing idly around when she went out to the patio. The former hoisted himself out when he saw her coming, seizing a towel to rub his hair as he moved to join her.

'You're looking a bit pale,' he observed, 'for someone with a touch of the sun.' His smile robbed the words of any sting. 'How do you feel?'

'Lethargic,' she admitted. 'I'll get over it.' She looked back at him steadily, wanting to get this over before Marion decided to join them. 'Why are you here, Brendon?'

'It's quite simple,' he said, making no attempt at prevarication. 'I told you I wouldn't give up that easily. Only if you can prove to me that you and Mark are really meant for each other shall I consider leaving you alone. And I'm going to take some convincing, believe me.'

'If you really meant what you said about loving me ——' she began, and saw his head move in swift negation.

'That won't work either. I know how I feel—just as I know how I can make you feel given half a chance. Mark whipped you away from me because he knew it too. There was no way he was going to let me take over. He's the only one allowed to do that sort of thing. It's Marion he should be married to.'

Dana's glance went briefly to the woman still in the water. 'Is that why you brought her along, to remind him what he's missing?'

'In a manner of speaking. At twenty-seven she's far more his weight, just as I'm more yours.' His tone softened. 'We had fun, Dana, as well as all the rest. Can you honestly say you ever laughed with Mark the way we laughed together?'

'No,' she was bound to admit, 'but that isn't to say it couldn't happen given the same situations.' She paused, eyes dark. 'Supposing I told you I was very much in love with your brother and perfectly happy with things the way they are? Would you believe that?'

'No, because it isn't true. Anyone looking at you could see it wasn't.' He shook his head decisively. 'I'm here and I'm staying. We both are. No matter what it takes, I'm going to put that sparkle back where it belongs.'

He could do that by taking Marion away again, she thought, and knew it wasn't that simple. Her reluctance to tell Mark about the baby stemmed from the same root cause: she was afraid of rejection. All Marion had done was bring that fear to a head by presenting her with a rival for his attention.

A rival worthy of attention, she had to concede as the

other came out of the water to reveal an excellent figure in the one-piece swimsuit. More Mark's weight, Brendon had said, and although he hadn't meant it so much physically as mentally, the former held true too. Marion was his equal in every respect—the kind of balance a man like Mark needed. And she loved him; the fact that she was here at all proved that much. Any woman willing to sink her pride so far over a man surely deserved to get him in the end.

CHAPTER ELEVEN

MARK came home late looking tired and harassed. 'I think it might be worth going into the economics of building our own canning factory,' he said over supper. 'At least that way we'd be able to control prices. The way things are going it should pay for itself in a relatively short time.'

'I had the same idea,' Brendon admitted. 'Only I got this notion that I needed a change of scene so I didn't do anything about it beyond sounding out the powers that be on the likelihood of planning permission. There shouldn't be too much difficulty if you go about it the right way.'

His brother looked at him for a long hard moment. 'Do you have a yen to get back in on the job?' he asked at length.

'Who, me?' Brendon shook his head. 'No, thanks, it's all yours. I'm here strictly for personal reasons.' His smile made light of the words. 'At least we'll be some company for Dana. She must have been bored half out of her mind the last couple of weeks if you and Gary have both been tied up.'

Blue eyes sought green, the former enigmatic. 'Have you been bored?'

'A little,' she was forced to acknowledge. 'I'll have to learn to drive, then I can get around on my own.'

'I'll teach you,' Brendon offered. 'You'd pick it up in no time—especially on automatic gears.'

It was Gary who asked the obvious question, speaking for the first time since they had sat down to the meal. 'Exactly how long do you plan on being here?'

'Haven't made any set plans,' came the easy admittance. 'I've time to kill till my new job starts in May. I'm going back into advertising—replacement for a guy who's retiring. Not quite top of the ladder, but it's a good enough start.'

'You always had a flair for it,' said Gary. 'Good luck, anyway.'

'Thanks. I need all I can get.' His glance came back to Dana before moving on to Mark. 'So what about these driving lessons? You've no objections?'

'It's entirely up to Dana,' he said without expression. 'Why not ask her?'

She answered before the question could be put again, conscious of his lack of interest. 'I'd like it. It might even be fun.' Her choice of words was deliberate. 'When can we start?'

'Tomorrow, if you like—unless Marion wants to go into town?'

'Count me out,' said the other girl. 'I'm more than content to just laze around here while I have the opportunity. I can't remember the last proper holiday I took.'

'Two years ago,' Mark put in. 'You went to Corsica.'

She smiled suddenly. 'So I did. You have a very good memory, Mark. Not that I enjoyed it so much on my own.'

'I never did find out what it is you do, Marion,' said Dana, surprising herself because she hadn't consciously intended to speak. She tagged on swiftly, 'Obviously it's a job of some importance.'

'To some.' The tone was light. 'I work for a firm of financial advisers.'

'Of which she's already a director,' Brendon added. 'You didn't know about that, did you, Mark?'

'No, I didn't.' He was looking at her with an odd expression. 'Congratulations. You deserve it.'

There was a certain wry quality to her smile. 'It's strange how you think you know exactly what you want and where you're going until you get there. The trouble is the challenge has gone out of it.'

'Then find another,' he suggested.

'I intend to,' she said.

She had found it already, thought Dana numbly. And this time she would be single-minded in the pursuit. She and Brendon were a pair in that respect if in no other way. What they wanted they went all out for, regardless of who or what stood in the way. Had it not been for the changes even now taking place inside her she might have felt tempted to sit back and let matters take their course—to let Mark do the choosing himself: she loved him enough to give him up. But for the baby's sake she had to make a fight of it, and the first step was to tell him what was happening to her. Only not quite yet, because she couldn't bear to see the look in his eyes when he realised he was trapped.

She slipped away early by pleading tiredness, once again pretending to be asleep when Mark came in. That she could rouse him to passion still if she set her mind to it she had no doubt, but without his love what did it really mean? At least he had been honest with her; he had never said he loved her in so many words. Had she not pushed him into it that fateful night he would probably never have touched her. She had brought the whole situation on them both.

He lay on his back with space between them when he eventually got into bed. In the ensuing silence, Dana could hear the sound of her own breathing, ragged and unnatural.

'You don't have to make believe you're asleep,' he said softly. 'I'm not coming near you. I think we both know now what's been missing from this marriage of ours. Sometimes it takes a shock to bring the truth home.'

Like the unexpected sight of someone you believed you'd put out of your mind for good, Dana thought achingly. He had tried so hard to make things work for them, but nothing could overcome the fact of her inadequacies.

'You can't love someone to order,' she said through the tightness in her throat, 'no matter how much you might want to. What are we going to do, Mark?'

'I'm not sure,' he admitted. He sounded totally flat and unemotional. 'I know I said I wouldn't be prepared to think about changing things for a couple of years or so, but circumstances alter. For the present we'd better just carry on the way we are. I don't want to make any more mistakes.'

It was a reprieve of sorts, but not for long. Somehow Dana had to find the courage to tell him the secret she carried. Where they would go from there she had no clear idea at all. The alternatives were few, and none of them acceptable.

The initial driving lessons were confined to the plantation roads, and provided a welcome relief from the problems besetting her. Brendon proved to be a rather surprisingly good teacher, neither too impatient nor too cautious. They used the plantation runabout because the smaller size gave Dana more confidence, and soon became a familiar sight bowling along between the fields of pineapple.

With authority to venture out on to the island roads, they began to go farther afield, although Dana still lacked the nerve to venture into Kahului itself. Even when asked, Marion declined to accompany them, on the grounds that a third person could prove more nerve-racking for the learner than anything.

Dana wanted to believe her, yet could not help suspecting an ulterior motive in the other girl's apparent willingness to be left alone. It was even possible that Mark was returning to the house himself during their absence just to be with her for a little while, but she refused to start varying their timetable in order to catch

him at it. Eventually something was going to have to be
done about the situation, but it became more and more
difficult as the days passed. They shared a room, they
slept in the same bed; in all other respects they were
miles apart.

It was Brendon who took her to meet Judy Wallman.
The Wallmans lived on the far side of Kahului in a
rambling, Colonial style house far too large for a couple
but which Judy wryly admitted she couldn't bear to
leave. English by birth, she was an attractive woman in
her mid-thirties whose American husband actually
worked on Oahu but preferred to commute on a daily
basis via inter-island air service.

Less hassle than travelling into L.A. from the place
they used to live, she confided in the manner of one well
accustomed to answering that particular question before
it was asked.

'I'd have contacted you before this,' she said apolo-
getically over coffee on the veranda with its magnificent
view over the Pacific, 'but Bob gained the impression
your husband needed time to get on top of the mess
Saul Rogers left before you started socialising. I don't
know what you were thinking of giving him the job in
the first place, Bren. He was little better than a drifter.'

'He was the only one available at the time,' Brendon
admitted without particular concern, 'and I was pretty
desperate to get away. I knew Mark was planning on
coming out early in the New Year, so there didn't seem
much chance of anything going radically wrong.'

'Well, you miscalculated.' Judy was obviously not one
to allow a subject to be dropped so easily. 'The man
was useless. Anyway, I understand your brother is well
on the way to solving all the problems. I only ever met
him once when he was out here a year or two ago.
Obviously a man to get things done, although I didn't
see him taking over on a permanent basis.' Her gaze
came back to Dana. 'You can't have been having much

of a time of it since you got here. If I get some people over tomorrow evening do you think you could persuade Mark to come and meet them?'

'I'm sure he'd be delighted,' Dana acknowledged, too well aware that he would be anything but. 'We have a guest staying. Will it be all right if I bring her along?'

'Of course. The more the merrier.' To Brendon she added, 'What about your younger brother? Is he a party man?'

'Gary's been ill,' put in Dana swiftly, afraid of what Brendon might say. 'It will depend on how he feels.'

'Well, he's welcome anyway. You all are.' If Judy had any curiosity at all as the exact nature of the said illness she was keeping it to herself. 'About eight, then.'

'Judy's a good sort,' Brendon commented when they were in the car and heading homewards. 'She looked after me when I first came out three years ago.'

'But you'd been here before, hadn't you?' said Dana.

'As a boy, and only for holidays. Grandfather was alive then. He was quite a character.'

'You're all characters,' she said almost to herself. There was a pause before she added tentatively, 'Brendon, the man you left in charge. Was it deliberate?'

He smiled wryly. 'Quick, aren't you? To be honest, I'm not even sure. I suppose I could have found someone more suitable if I'd really put my mind to it. I had this suspicion that Mark had a hankering to take over the plantation himself. Maybe subconsciously I wanted to make things as difficult as possible for him.' His tone altered slightly. 'Strange how things pan out. If I'd married Marion three years ago I wonder where I'd be now.'

'Happily domesticated,' she suggested, and saw the smile come again.

'I doubt it. Marion and domesticity don't go together. She didn't want children, for one thing. At the time I went along with that idea—now I'm not so sure. I suppose it has to depend on circumstances as much as anything. With the right kind of wife a man could take pleasure in creating a family.' He gave her a swift glance. 'I'm talking about you, Dana. You'd make a fine mother.'

It was someone outside of herself who replied to that. 'I daresay I might some day. Do you realise it's almost twelve-thirty, by the way? They'll have started lunch by the time we get back.'

'So we called on a friend and lost track of time,' he came back unperturbed. 'It's only the truth. Anyway, Mark may not have come home to lunch. Grandfather had the company offices based in town because it was his firm belief that popping home in the middle of the day simply unsettled him for the rest of it. Mark seems to share that view, from what I've seen.'

'Not today,' she said. 'He was visiting the sorting sheds in the north section this morning.'

'Well, Marion will have kept him entertained. They speak the same language, those two. I should have realised that years ago.' He pulled over in order to give an oncoming car more room on the narrow roadway, adding levelly, 'I think it's time we started thinking about the future from all viewpoints, don't you? How much longer can you go on living with a man you don't have anything in common with? There's nothing binding you—nothing irremediable anyway. True, a divorce could take a couple of years, unless Mark could be persuaded to give you adequate grounds. I'd say he owed you that much for making an annulment impossible in the first place.'

'What makes you so sure Mark would contemplate a divorce at all?' Dana asked, playing for time.

'Because he's no happier with the situation as it is than you are. That has to be obvious to anyone seeing the two of you together.' He hesitated. 'You're not still sleeping together, are you?'

'No,' she responded dully. 'Not in the sense you mean.' The damage, she could have added, was already done. She didn't because there was no way she could tell Brendon the truth of the matter without first telling Mark. Which brought her right back to square one. The decision was hers and hers alone. No one could help her. Sometimes she felt like a caged animal running round in circles trying to find a way out.

It was five minutes to one when they reached the house. Mark and Marion were out on the patio finishing pre-lunch drinks, the latter bandbox-fresh and smoothly attractive in a short-sleeved linen which made Dana doubly conscious of her own crumpled cotton. Had she possessed the confidence befitting her supposed position in the household, she could have ordered lunch to be held back for a few minutes while she went and changed. The way things were she simply accepted the situation.

Brendon made the necessary explanations, his tone airy, as if three hours' absence instead of the one announced was of no particular consequence.

'Judy wants us all to go over there tomorrow night for a bit of a get-together,' he finished as Lani came out to announce that the meal was ready to be served.

Mark was looking at Dana, expression enigmatic. 'What did you tell her?'

She met the blue eyes with only the faintest flicker of her own. 'What would you expect me to have told her? I said we'd be delighted, of course.'

'Which doesn't really leave any choice.' Marion put a slim-fingered hand on his arm, her smile understanding. 'It might not be as bad as it sounds—and you certainly could do with a break.'

The answering smile was reluctant. 'As you say, there isn't much choice. I just didn't want to get in on that particular scene yet.'

Because of her? Dana wondered. Because he couldn't bring himself to face the kind of speculation their relationship invariably aroused? She knew that was only half the answer. Had their marriage been a good one he wouldn't have cared what anyone thought.

Mark went back to work straight after the meal, leaving the three of them to their individual devices. Tired, and feeling the heat, Dana went to lie down for half an hour, making the excuse that she had a letter to write. She did actually contemplate dropping a line to Beverley, but the sheer effort entailed was too much. What could she say, in any case? What was left to say?

It was gone four when she awoke, and the light was already beginning to assume the deeper golden glow of evening. She felt totally unrested, her head heavy. With the thought that a swim might help to refresh her, she got into a suit and went out to the pool, refusing to be deterred by the sight of Marion already in the water. She could hardly go on avoiding a confrontation for ever.

The other girl was out of the pool and drying herself on a towel when Dana surfaced from her dive. She did a couple of lengths without any great enthusiasm and emerged with even less. This was the first time she had found herself entirely alone with the older woman. She barely knew what to say to her.

Marion took the problem out of her hands by speaking first. 'Brendon went into town about an hour ago. He said to tell you he wouldn't be long.' She paused, her smile a little ironic. 'You know he's in love with you, don't you?'

'I know he says he is,' Dana replied with care, wrapping her towel about her shoulders. 'I'm still not sure who he's trying to convince.'

'Oh, you can take his word for it. I've never known him this intense about anything before.'

'Including yourself?' Dana regretted the words the moment they left her lips. 'I'm sorry,' she tagged on impulsively. 'That was uncalled-for.'

'The answer is yes, anyhow.' The other girl sounded unmoved. 'Brendon and I were never really suited.'

'Especially not after you met Mark.' This time Dana took pains to keep her tone steady. 'Only you wanted your career too, and he wasn't prepared to share.'

Marion's expression had undergone a subtle change. 'He told you that?'

'Yes, he told me. If it's any consolation, he also told me he was on the verge of changing his mind when he—met me.'

'And was forced into marrying you instead.'

Dana was very still, her only sign of life in the pulse beating rapidly at her temple. 'How did you know?' she got out at last, and scarcely needed to be told the answer.

'Brendon gave me the whole story before we came out here. It's the main reason I'm here. You see, until that moment I'd genuinely believed Mark had chosen you in preference to me.'

'Brendon had no right.' The words came out thickly.

Marion's shrug contradicted that statement. 'I don't see why not. After all, it isn't as if you and Mark are happy together. He was a fool to complicate matters the way he did, but I suppose he felt he had to make every effort towards making the marriage work. He even gave up a whole way of life to that purpose.'

Dana's eyes had gone dark. 'He'd been planning to do that for years. He didn't want to hurt his father, that's . . .' Her voice died away in the face of open scepticism. 'Ask him,' she finished lamely.

'I don't need to ask him,' Marion said with confidence. 'I know how he felt about the bank. It should have been *his* bank now, and would have been if he hadn't had this need to get away from all the talk. A man who marries a girl so much younger than himself comes in for a lot of flak—especially a man in his position. You left him no alternative.'

Dana felt sick. While she still did not wholly believe it, there was enough plausibility in Marion's reasoning to lend some credence.

'Supposing you're right,' she said on a husky note, 'what would you suggest I do about it?'

The reply was a moment in coming. 'That has to be up to you,' Marion stated at length. 'Brendon would take you away like a shot if you gave him half a chance.'

If it weren't for one thing she would go too, Dana thought bleakly. A fresh start was what they all needed. She had cost Mark the chairmanship, but without her he could still go back. This wasn't his kind of life; she wasn't his kind of woman. The cage was growing ever smaller.

Judy's few people turned out to be a mixed bag of a dozen or more, ranging from Joe and Ellen Harper who had retired to the islands fairly recently, down to Tracy Williams, the twenty-year-old daughter of the local medical practitioner.

'I was told there was a younger brother around my age,' she said to Dana at one point when they found themselves temporarily isolated from the rest of the gathering. Her laugh was totally without selfconsciousness. 'Most of the boys I meet are here on vacation. I was looking forward to getting to know one who wouldn't be leaving at the end of the week. Didn't he want to come?'

'He didn't feel in the mood for meeting new people,' Dana admitted with truth, adding on a confiding note, 'Actually, I think he imagined it was going to be strictly a middle-aged affair.'

'You hardly come into that category yourself,' Tracy pointed out. 'You're younger than I am, aren't you?'

'A little.' Dana had no intention of enlarging on that. 'Sisters-in-law don't count.'

'Nor brothers, by the look of it. Your husband isn't exactly decrepit.' Her glance rested with approval on Brendon who was talking with Judy and another man a few yards away. 'He's very attractive. Does Gary resemble him at all?'

The silence went on too long; Dana knew she was going to have to say it. 'Brendon isn't my husband,' she stated expressionlessly. 'I'm married to Mark.'

'Mark?' There was no attempt to conceal the astonishment. 'Oh, but I thought . . . I mean . . .' She stopped, the laugh this time more than a little wry. 'To tell you the truth, I got the impression he was with the blonde—Marion, isn't it? Sorry about that. I can't have been listening properly when Judy was introducing you all.' Curiosity was already overcoming the faint discomfiture, her gaze now searching for and fastening on to the other man on the far side of the room. 'He's a lot older than you, isn't he? How did you meet?'

'He was a business acquaintance of my father's.' Dana made a small gesture of appeal to Brendon as he turned his eyes momentarily in their direction. Tracy was not the kind to have many reservations when it came to asking probing questions. The last thing she wanted was to be on the receiving end.

To her infinite relief her plea for aid was answered. Brendon said something to his companions, then came on over.

'Hi,' he greeted them cheerfully. 'What are the two prettiest females in the room doing skulking in a corner? It's Tracy, isn't it? I was talking with your father a few minutes ago. I hear you're planning on going to medical school yourself.'

'Thinking about it,' she corrected. 'I haven't been accepted yet.' She shrugged. 'Even if I am I'm not sure *I'll* accept. I can't really make up my mind.'

'Then it certainly does need thinking about,' he agreed.

'Tracy was hoping to see Gary here,' Dana put in. 'Perhaps we should have tried harder to persuade him.'

'Not easy these days once he sets his mind to something.' Brendon smiled at the girl. 'Why don't you come over to the house this weekend if it's company you're looking for? You'd be more than welcome.'

'I might do that,' she said. 'There's Mom waving. I'd better go and see what she wants.' She sounded resigned. 'Maybe what I really need is a complete break away from all things family!'

'Something of a self-centred young woman,' commented Brendon dryly when she was out of earshot. 'I doubt if she's the right material for a doctor anyhow.' He studied Dana for a moment, his manner altering. 'You look a bit pale. Are you feeling okay?'

'I have a headache,' she admitted. 'I think it must be all the smoke in here.'

'You need some fresh air,' he said with authority. 'Come on out to the veranda. It's a lovely night after that rain we had on the way here.'

It was indeed a lovely night, the breeze just fresh enough without being chilly. Dana leaned on the rail to look out over scattering rooftops to the vast expanse that was the Pacific, palely lit by a crescent moon. In a few days she would have been married to Mark for three whole months, and where had it got her? One thing was certain, she could go on like this no longer. Tonight she was going to tell him the truth and let him face the problem along with her.

'I hate seeing you in this state,' Brendon said softly from close by her side. 'You're hardly the same girl any more. The worst thing Mark could have done was to bring you out here. There's nothing for you.'

There could have been so much, she reflected painfully, had he only loved her. She shivered suddenly despite the warmth of the air, and felt Brendon's arm come protectively about her shoulders.

'You can't carry on like this,' he said, unconsciously echoing her thoughts of a moment before. 'Dana, come back to England with me. Let me give you a taste of the life a girl your age should be enjoying. You're not doing anyone any good by sticking it out.'

'Two years is a long time to wait,' she murmured. 'Would you be prepared to wait, Brendon?'

'If necessary—although I'm not saying it would be easy.' The arm firmed, turning her towards him, his hands coming up to cup her face between the palms with a gentleness that made her want to weep. 'Dana, I love you. I want to see you happy. I think—no, I know I can make you happy. Just give me the opportunity.'

'Can we talk about it some other time?' she asked in quiet desperation. 'It just doesn't feel right to be discussing something like this on someone else's veranda.'

'An abuse of hospitality, you mean?' He sighed, and took his hands away. 'I suppose you're right. Only I'm not going back to ignoring the whole subject either. Do you realise I haven't even kissed you since I got here?'

After tomorrow he might not even want to, she told herself. The fact that she was carrying Mark's child had to make a difference to his feelings for her.

'I want to go back inside,' she said. 'Please, Brendon.'

Mark was standing in direct line with the veranda doors when they entered the room. His glance was fleeting, his attention to the conversation at present in progress apparently undisturbed as he made some smiling reply to the woman standing opposite, yet Dana could sense the coldness in him. She felt cold herself, not physically but emotionally. She wished they could go home now and get it over with. Anything had to be better than this limbo she had created.

During the following hour or so she spoke with several people, including Tracy's parents, who turned out to be an exceedingly pleasant couple.

'I suppose you've realised I'm the local quack,' joked

Doctor Jackson. 'At least with someone your age I'm unlikely to be asked for a free consultation!' He smiled and lifted his shoulders at his wife's admonishing murmur. 'It happens all the time at functions like this one. I spend the evening listening to recitals of symptoms. Your husband was telling me he used to get the same thing, except that with him it was financial advice, of course. He's a wise man to make his escape while he still has his best years ahead of him. This is a fine climate for bringing up a family.'

Could he have guessed? Dana wondered, feeling her jaw tense involuntarily as she met the twinkling eyes. Lani had, but that had been nothing to do with medical foresight.

'I'll bear it in mind,' she promised on as light a note as she could manage.

There were several smokers in the room, most of them with cigars. Unaccustomed to the smell and taste as the Senior men rarely indulged, Dana eventually began to find it overwhelming. So far nausea had struck her only in the mornings, and at an hour when she had been able to conceal it from Mark. To succumb to it here would not only spoil Judy's party but possibly reveal her secret before she was ready to do so. She had to get outside, she told herself urgently.

Brendon was engaged in conversation some distance away, his back turned towards her. Murmuring an excuse to the people she was with, she made her way over to the veranda doors, stepping out into the night air with an indrawn breath of sheer relief. That was better already. Why on earth people felt the need to congregate indoors in this climate she failed to understand. True, the temperature was probably low by Hawaiian standards. It was all a matter of what one was accustomed to.

The veranda ran across the back of the house and down one side. Still feeling too queasy to venture back indoors, Dana strolled towards the corner, her footsteps noiseless on the artificial grass flooring the whole area. A cloud was passing across the moon. It could rain again before morning. After April it would be summer once more; there were only two seasons in this part of the world, and those fairly ill-defined. Would she still be here then? he wondered. Was there, in fact, any choice?

There was someone else out here, she realised suddenly, hearing the sound of a woman's voice speaking softly. She paused, not wanting to break in on any private conversation going on around the corner, and was about to turn and retrace her steps when a male voice replied, freezing her where she stood.

'This isn't doing either of us any good. I think we'd better go back indoors.'

Dana came back to life with a jerk. In another moment Mark and Marion would come round the corner and see her. What would they say? What would she say? The time for facing up to things was not yet.

There were steps leading down into the gardens just a few feet away. She reached them in seconds, no longer quite rational in her desire to escape. The wood was damp from the previous rain, her leather-soled sandals too smooth underneath to give her secure footing. She felt herself start to skid and made a desperate but futile grab for the handrail, and the darkness came up to meet her.

CHAPTER TWELVE

THE sun was shining when she awoke, although the drawn blinds muted the light to a comfortable degree. An unfamiliar room, she realised in momentary disorientation, then memory started coming back and with it a sense of loss so deep she wanted just to close her eyes and shut the knowledge out again.

There was a movement somewhere in the room, and Judy Wallman came into her line of vision, her smile over-bright.

'Hi!' she said. 'How are you feeling?'

'Empty,' Dana told her, and thought that the word accurately described both mind and body. Even her voice sounded dead. 'I lost the baby, didn't I?'

'I'm afraid so.' The brightness had vanished, sympathy taking its place. 'You had a very bad fall. There was nothing Jim could do. He only left a couple of hours ago. He said to tell you there was absolutely no reason why you shouldn't have a dozen babies if you want them. You're young and in perfect health and . . .'

'It's all right, Judy.' Dana said it softly, aware of the woman's very real distress. 'I can cope.' She hesitated, reluctant to ask the most obvious question. 'Is Mark here?'

'Of course. He went to get some breakfast not fifteen minutes ago. I'll fetch him, shall I?'

'No, not just yet. Let him finish eating.' That moment, Dana thought, would come soon enough. 'How has he taken it?'

'Very hard.' It was Judy's turn to hesitate. 'He didn't know, did he? About the baby, I mean.'

'No,' Dana admitted, and felt the need for some explanation. 'I wanted to be quite sure before I told him. I was going to go and see Dr Jackson this week.'

'According to Jim you should have seen him a couple of weeks ago. Not that it would have made any difference in this case, of course.' Judy added wryly, 'I feel particularly bad that it was our steps you fell down.'

'Then you mustn't. My foot slipped, that's all. It could have happened just as easily anywhere else.'

'I'll try to remember that.' Judy briskened. 'Look, I'm going to fetch Mark. He said I was to if you woke up before he got back. You'll be okay?'

'Of course.' Dana managed a weak smile. 'I'm going to be fine.'

Judy smiled back, not deceived. 'That's the spirit!'

Dana hung on grimly to her self-control as the door closed, determined not to give way to the tears which threatened to choke her. What was there to weep about anyway? She should be feeling relief. She had found the solution she had been looking for.

Mark came within minutes. He had shaved, but looked tired and drawn, his eyes dull. He didn't touch her, not even to take her hand, standing there at the side of the bed to look down at her pale face in its frame of lank and lifeless hair.

'Why didn't you tell me?' he asked. 'You did know, didn't you? You had to have known.'

'Yes, I knew.' Her voice was scarcely more than a whisper. 'It should be obvious why I didn't tell you, Mark.'

'Because of the complications? Because it tied us together?' Every word was forced out. 'There had to be a better solution than this!'

She stared at him for whole seconds before it finally got through to her. 'I didn't,' she cried. 'Mark, it was an accident!'

'Was it?' He sounded unconvinced. 'I blame myself

for letting things get this far. I should have stuck it out from the word go.'

'Mark . . .' she put out a hand towards him appealingly . . . 'please!'

'What else am I to think?' he demanded. 'Jim Jackson warned me to expect a great deal of distress when you woke. He even left tranquillisers to calm you down. But you hardly need them, do you, Dana? You're as calm as if it had never happened.'

Not calm, she wanted to say, just numb. She didn't because it wasn't going to be any use. He had made up his mind and nothing was going to shake him. She turned her face away from him. 'What are we going to do?' she got out.

'We'll talk about that later,' he said. 'Jim is coming back to see you this afternoon. You were lucky you didn't break anything. You fell the whole way down those steps.' For the first time he took hold of her hand, but it was only to tuck it under the cover. He seemed to be holding himself rigidly in check. 'Do you hurt anywhere?'

She hurt everywhere and in every sense, but nothing would have dragged the admission from her. 'I can cope,' she said, using the same words she had used to Judy a short time ago. 'Just leave me alone, will you, Mark? I want to be left alone!'

He went without argument, as if he too couldn't wait to be finished with the whole dreadful business. Even then she couldn't let go. The pain went too deep for tears to ease.

It was to be a further forty-eight hours before Dr Jackson would allow her to move back home to the plantation, and at that the bruising to her back and limbs made the journey far from comfortable. Mark said little during the drive, his manner withdrawn. A tangible barrier lay between them; Dana doubted if anyone or anything could ever break it down now.

She had not seen Brendon since the night of the party. The sight of him brought little reaction; she felt little reaction to anything these days. He himself seemed subdued, his greeting cautious.

'You gave us all a scare,' he told her. 'Good thing Jim was on the spot.'

'Wasn't it,' Mark agreed for her. The blue eyes were emotionless. 'If you're feeling all right I'll go back to town. I've some people to see.'

It was neither better nor worse when he had gone. At Brendon's suggestion, they went out to the patio, where he insisted she take a lounger. Dana did so because it wasn't worth disputing the point, lying back in the shade of the umbrella with closed eyes.

'Where's Marion?' she asked.

'She left yesterday.' Brendon sounded as if he were under some strain. 'She didn't give me any details, just said she and Mark had reached an understanding.' The pause was lengthy. When he spoke again it was on a different note. 'He and I had a long talk ourselves last night—the first in years.'

'About what?'

'You.' He added slowly, 'The basis is that if you're willing to come back to England with me he's willing to let you go. Everything above board, of course. You'll have your own place. I finally managed to convince him that my motives concerning you are purely honourable.'

What kind of understanding? Dana wondered, barely listening to the rest. Was Marion to come back here when she had gone, or was Mark to go to her? Either way, it wasn't going to matter very much. She needed to get away as much as he obviously wanted her out of the way.

'Dana?' Brendon was watching her with uncertainty. 'Did you hear what I just said?'

'I heard.' She turned her head towards him, gave him a faint smile. 'Mark thinks I let myself fall down those steps on purpose because I didn't want the baby. Do you think that too?'

'No, I don't,' he came back with conviction. 'You're incapable of anything like that.'

'Thank you.' The acknowledgement was soft. 'Personally, I can't wait to leave.'

Wisely Brendon retained his distance, the answering smile indicative of his feelings. 'As soon as possible, then. You won't be sorry, Dana. I'm going to make up to you for all this.'

'I'll need a job,' she said, and saw him hesitate.

'I don't think Mark is going to go along with that idea. As long as you're still married to him he aims to go on maintaining you.'

'I can't live off him for two years,' Dana protested without any great display of emotion.

'You won't have to if everything goes according to plan.' Brendon was sitting on the extreme edge of his chair, eager to convince her. 'In six months he's prepared to let you divorce him on grounds he'll supply. Uncontested, it would be through in as little as six weeks. You won't even have to go to court. After that you'd be my responsibility.'

Everybody's but her own, she thought. There was one alternative. She could go back to Aunt Eleanor's. In helping the latter run her charitable organisations she would at least be earning her keep. If Brendon loved her and wanted her as much as he said he did he would accept that arrangement for as long as necessary. And afterwards? Well, that would have to be decided. Right now she felt she had had enough of marriage to last her a lifetime.

'We'll talk about it,' she said, and sat up to swing her feet to the ground. 'I'm going to change. This dress is far too warm.'

It was no surprise to find that Mark had moved his things from the room they had shared. They could hardly have gone on doing so. Her face in the bathroom mirror looked pinched and colourless, her eyes lacklustre. No stranger meeting her for the first time would take her now for merely eighteen, she thought depressedly. She had aged years. It said a lot for the strength of Brendon's regard that he could see her like this and still feel the same.

She made an effort that evening, donning her most becoming dress and using a touch of shadow on her lids to supply the lacking sparkle. At her own request they were eating out of doors tonight because she couldn't bear the thought of being cooped up inside. Gary was already seated at the poolside bar with a drink when she went out.

'I'm sorry,' he said without beating about the bush. 'I really am sorry, Dana. I suppose you're sick of people telling you there's always another time.'

'Not for Mark and me,' she returned without inflection. 'I'm leaving.' She looked at him for a moment. 'You don't seem surprised.'

'I'm not,' he admitted. 'It was going wrong before this happened. In some ways it was ...' He broke off abruptly, shaking his head. 'Forget it.'

'You were going to say in some ways it was as well it did happen,' she supplied. 'As a matter of fact, I agree with you.' She closed her heart and her mind to the shaft of pain which repudiated that statement. 'A child should never be the one thing holding a marriage together.'

Mark and Brendon came out from the house together before Gary could reply—if he had been considering a reply. Had they, Dana wondered with newly acquired cynicism, been discussing her future again? Everything had been taken into account except her feelings on the subject. It was perhaps time they both realised she had a mind of her own.

It was not an easy evening, although both Brendon

and Gary did their best to lighten the atmosphere. Mark's suggestion that she had an early night was accepted by Dana without demur. There was little point in prolonging the agony beyond the absolutely necessary. With her gone, the three men might be able to relax.

She had been only two or three minutes in the bedroom when the tap came on the door. Although she had half expected it, it still made her heart jerk. Mark entered quietly in answer to her call, closing the door again to stand with his back to it but not touching.

'There are things we have to discuss,' he said. 'This seems to be the most private place to do it.'

Dana remained standing too, allowing herself no weakening of resolve. 'If you're going to tell me what you and Brendon have already decided you don't have to bother. He did it for you.'

'Did he?' The blue eyes narrowed just a fraction. 'And how do you feel about it?'

'I'm quite ready to go home,' she said, 'but when I do it will be to Aunt Eleanor's.'

'You weren't happy there before,' he pointed out. 'What makes you think this time will be any better?'

'Because it couldn't be worse than living here with you.' She wasn't trying to hurt him, simply stating a fact. She doubted anyway if anything she said could hurt him very deeply. One had to care to be hurt. No, that wasn't quite fair, was it? He cared enough to be concerned for her future welfare. 'I can't keep on living off you,' she added. 'Can't you understand that?'

'I understand it, even if I don't like it.' He paused, a muscle tensing in his jaw. 'What about Brendon?'

For the first time she looked him squarely in the face, taking in the new lines of strain about the mouth and eyes. There was still no feeling in her.

'Brendon believes in me,' she said. 'He's what I need.

I should have appreciated that weeks ago then none of this would have happened.'

'True,' he agreed. 'That seems to say it all, doesn't it?' He stirred himself to reach for the door handle again. 'You'd better give it the clear week before thinking about travelling. I'll leave it to Brendon to make the arrangements. Do you want me to cable your aunt?'

'I'll do it.' Her voice felt stuck in the back of her throat. 'Goodnight, Mark.'

His glance back at her held irony. 'Shouldn't that be goodbye?'

She sent the cable from town the following day, and had the reply in her hands twenty-four hours later. Succinct as usual, Aunt Eleanor had put it all in two short words: 'Come home'.

'It's so far out of town,' said Brendon when she showed it to him. 'I'm only going to get to see you weekends.'

'You can come and stay,' she invited. 'The house is big enough. Mind you, you'll probably get roped in for something. Aunt Eleanor takes advantage of every pair of hands, willing or unwilling. Anyway, it's that or nothing. Take it or leave it.'

'Oh, I'll take it,' he said resignedly. 'I don't have much choice.'

A lump came suddenly and painfully into her throat. 'Bren, wouldn't it be simpler if we just called the whole thing off? You'll find someone else.'

'Except that I don't want anybody else.' He kept his eyes on the road, looking at that moment more like Mark than ever. 'What do I have to do to prove it to you?'

'You don't have to prove anything to me,' she said thickly. 'Only just don't rush me. I'm nobody's property except my own.'

'Of course not.' He sounded subdued. 'I've booked a flight to L.A. on Thursday afternoon, and a couple of rooms overnight at the Hyatt. We're due in Heathrow ten o'clock Saturday morning.'

'Good.' There seemed nothing else to say. By the weekend this part of her life would be over. She need never see Mark again if she didn't want to. If eventually she married Brendon that was one thing he was going to have to understand from the start. No family involvement. She wanted to forget there had ever been an older brother.

Mark's decision to drive them to the airport on Thursday afternoon came out of the blue. Brendon made a half-hearted attempt to put him off the idea, but to no avail.

'Somebody has to get you there,' he pointed out, 'and I'm available. What difference does it make?'

It was Dana who answered, her voice as calm and uncaring as his. 'None at all. It's very kind of you, Mark.'

Just for a moment something sparked in his eyes, then he inclined his head in acknowledgement and the moment was gone. 'Let's get the waggon loaded,' he said.

Dana elected to sit in the rear of the station waggon, leaving Brendon to occupy the front passenger seat. She gazed fixedly out of the window the whole journey, ignoring, or trying to ignore, the sense of panic growing inside her. She would be all right once she was on the plane, she told herself over and over. Goodbyes were always traumatic, no matter what the circumstances. Another hour and all would be well.

She was rigidly in control of herself when they reached the airport, even managing a smile for the check-in clerk at the desk. With their luggage checked and boarding passes allocated it still wanted twenty minutes or so to boarding the plane itself. Mark suggested a coffee, obviously intending to stick it out to the bitter end.

It was hot and it was aromatic, but Dana couldn't drink hers. She felt as though something were slowly coming unravelled deep down inside. Mark was sitting next to her at the round table, lean, tanned hands only inches from hers when he took up his cup. Those hands knew her as well as hers knew him. He had taught her the importance of touch, the way he had taught her so many other things. What he had failed to tell her was how to make him love her, and now he never would. She was going away many thousands of miles to a land that held nothing for her, because everything she wanted was here.

The call to board the L.A. flight brought them all to their feet in unison. Dana kept her head down and her lips tight as they moved towards the gate, willing herself to carry it through without breaking down. The need to turn to him, to bury her face against his chest and cling was like a scream in her head. Yet outwardly she revealed nothing, her walk quite steady. Another few steps and they would be through. If she was going to turn back the time was now. Yet she kept on going. Mark had Marion. He had given her to Brendon. Turning back on that arrangement only complicated matters.

The leavetaking was brief, his farewell a mere touch on the lips which nevertheless left her aching. As usual it was impossible to read his thoughts as he looked down at her. 'Be happy,' he said. 'I'll be in touch.' Then he shook hands with Brendon and was gone, striding away across the concourse without a backward glance.

There was a lengthy walk across the tarmac to the waiting plane. Dana moved like an automaton, barely able to see through the tears welling in her eyes. It was Brendon who stopped, taking her gently by the arm and drawing her to one side to lift her face so he could see it. The pain in his expression was a direct reflection of her own deep-felt anguish.

'You love him, don't you?' he said. 'You really do love him.'

'I'm sorry,' she choked. 'I didn't mean to give way like this. I'll be all right once I get away from here.'

'I don't think so.' He paused, ignoring the curious stares of the other passengers, a sudden wry acceptance in the blue eyes so like his brother's. 'Dana, there was no point in telling you while I thought you wanted to leave Mark, but this has to alter things. He and Marion don't have any arrangement. He gave her her marching orders. The reason he's letting you go so easily is because he believes you're in love with me.' The wryness increased. 'I've been trying to convince myself that way too, only there comes a time when you have to face up to facts.'

Dana was gazing at him with hope faintly dawning in her heart, searching his features as if seeing them for the first time. 'What are you trying to say?' she whispered.

'That you should go back. That you should give it another chance. I'll have your stuff sent back from L.A.' He was smiling, but the smile nowhere reached his eyes. He kissed her once, a fleeting tribute, then he was turning her about and pushing her gently towards the doors through which passengers were still streaming. 'Go on, before I change my mind. He won't have left the airport yet.'

She looked back at him for a moment, the mist in her eyes this time for him. 'Thank you,' she said.

Mark was standing at one of the windows overlooking the main runway, his back to the throngs. He looked relaxed, like any other observer, his hands clasped behind his back in classic Duke of Edinburgh style. Only as Dana approached closer to him did she see the tension in those overlapping fingers, the whiteness of the knuckles where they clenched. He was waiting for their plane to take off, seeing it through to the very last moment. There was hope in that alone.

She said his name softly, seeing his shoulders stiffen. Then he turned and saw her and for the first time ever the mask was gone, stripped from him by an emotion so intense her every doubt vanished. Control came swiftly, but not swiftly enough.

'Did you forget something?' he asked.

'Yes.' She could hardly get the words out she was so full up. 'I forgot to tell you I love you, Mark. Will you take me home?'

They made the car with his arm wrapped so tightly about her she thought he would never let her go. Only when they were off the airport and safely on a side road did he pull in and cut out the engine, turning to her with a need that had to be assuaged.

'I thought I'd lost you,' he murmured roughly against her hair when that first desperately searching kiss was over. 'I thought it was Brendon you wanted.'

'And I thought you wanted Marion,' she said. 'That time we came back from the beach and found them there, you changed completely towards me.'

'Of course I did! How was I supposed to react when the very sight of Brendon sitting there with another woman made you sick to your stomach?' He paused, tone altering a little. 'If I'd known about the baby . . .'

'Oh, Mark, I'm so sorry.' She pressed her lips to his skin below the angle of his jaw, feeling the tension in him. 'I was afraid to tell you because I thought you wouldn't want that kind of tie.'

'If I'd felt that strongly about it I'd have made sure it didn't happen,' he returned. 'Dana, what I said the morning after your fall . . .'

'It isn't true,' she cut in. 'It really was an accident.'

'I know.' He held her away from him so that he could see her face, his own rueful. 'I was in shock myself, although I didn't realise it at the time. When I started thinking rationally again it was already too late. That's when I decided Brendon had to be better for you than I could ever be. He still is, if it comes to that.'

'It isn't Brendon I want,' she said. 'I'm very, very

fond of him and always will be, but compared with you . . .' she stopped and smiled . . . 'well, there is no comparison. I fell in love with you when I was sweet seventeen and I haven't stopped loving you since. Not even when I convinced myself that I had. Perhaps some of it was infatuation to start with, the way you told me it was, but I soon learned the difference. You know,' she added, 'in spite of everything I have to be grateful to my father. If he hadn't forced you into marrying me I'd never have known you.'

'I wasn't forced.' Mark was smiling a little as if in recollection. 'I could have refused to go along with what he was asking—that part of it, at least. I told myself I was only doing it for your sake, and made myself believe it too, when all the time I simply couldn't bear the thought of someone else having you. Do you remember that very first evening at your father's apartment? You were so fresh and unspoiled. I nearly agreed to that extension he was asking for on the strength of his daughter's appeal alone, except that I realised he was probably counting on just such a reaction. What I did do, of course, was far worse in the end.'

Dana was taking in about one word in three, her mind confused. 'I don't think I understand,' she said.

'It's quite simple. I wanted a girl half my age and I was ashamed of it, so I disguised it under the name of philanthropy. It worked up until the time I found out about Brendon, then jealousy took over. I'm afraid it blinded me to everything else.'

She gazed at him with eyes gone wide and disbelieving. 'You're saying it was all pretence? Even in Bembridge?'

'If you mean did I want to make love to you on our wedding night, the answer has to be yes, even though I wouldn't let myself admit it. That night we shared a bed nearly finished me!' He was silent for a moment watching her, his expression undergoing a subtle change: 'I'm still too old for you.'

'You're thirty-five,' she said. 'All right, nearly thirty-six. That's not old. Anyway, girls mature quickly once they start.'

'You had to do it too quickly.' His lips had thinned. 'Eighteen years old, and you've already suffered more than you should ever have to do.'

Dana said softly, 'You know what Dr Jackson told me the best therapy for my complaint was? To get myself pregnant again. I wanted to tell him what to do with his advice at the time, but now it seems to make sense. I want your baby, Mark.'

His eyes were very blue. 'Not quite yet. Give it another year. I want you to myself for a little while. Is that selfish?'

'No,' she said, 'just nice.' Her voice quivered suddenly, torn by an emotion she couldn't contain. 'Take me home, Mark. It's where we both belong.'

Harlequin® Plus
A HAWAIIAN FEAST

If you are lucky enough to visit Hawaii, you would doubtless have the pleasure of attending a *lu'au*, the traditional Hawaiian feast. If you live in Hawaii, you'd probably at some time or other give your own *lu'au*—and this is how you'd do it . . . .

First, invite about sixty for dinner, for what's a *lu'au* without lots of people! The main item on the menu is pork—but very special pork. Purchase the carcass of a ninety-pound whole pig, have it cleaned and shaved, then rubbed inside with salt and soya sauce. The pig is then cooked in an *imu*.

To make an *imu*, dig a hole in the ground, a foot and a half deep and long enough for the pig. Build a roaring fire in the hole and add about two dozen *imu* stones— porous rocks about four inches in diameter. After three or four hours, put the red-hot rocks inside the pig, truss the pig, line the pit with banana leaves, add the pig (upside down) and throw in a crateful of scrubbed sweet potatoes. Cover the mound with earth to keep in the steam and cook for about four hours.

When it's ready, serve with *poi*, a Hawaiian staple made of ground taro leaves, or perhaps with some *mahimahi*, a kind of cooked fish. For dessert, *haupia*, or coconut pudding, is popular, although many people like to just nibble on bananas, pineapples, papayas and mangoes.

An indispensable part of the *lu'au* is the soft music of the ukelele, playing songs of the South Pacific. You also need warm sea breezes nudging the palm trees and a crimson sun ducking below the ocean horizon. Order up all these ingredients, and you have one very successful *lu'au*.

Aloha!

Legacy of PASSION

BY CATHERINE KAY

A love story begun long ago comes full circle...

Venice, 1819: Contessa Allegra di Rienzi, young, innocent, unhappily married. She gave her love to Lord Byron—scandalous, irresistible English poet. Their brief, tempestuous affair left her with a shattered heart, a few poignant mementos—and a daughter he never knew about.

Boston, today: Allegra Brent, modern, independent, restless. She learned the secret of her great-great-great-grandmother and journeyed to Venice to find the di Rienzi heirs. There she met the handsome, cynical, blood-stirring Conte Renaldo di Rienzi, and like her ancestor before her, recklessly, hopelessly lost her heart.

What the press says about Harlequin romance fiction...

"When it comes to romantic novels...
Harlequin is the indisputable king."
— *New York Times*

"'Harlequin [is]...the best and the biggest.'"
— *Associated Press* (quoting Janet Dailey's husband, Bill)

"The most popular reading matter of
American women today."
— *Detroit News*

"...exciting escapism, easy reading, interesting
characters and, always, a happy ending....
They are hard to put down."
— *Transcript-Telegram*, Holyoke (Mass.)

"...a work of art."
— *Globe & Mail*, Toronto